Dorothy's Derby Chronicles

Rise of the
Undead
Redhead

Author/Illustrations Copyright © 2014 by Meghan Dougherty
and Alece Birnbach
Cover and internal design © 2014 by Sourcebooks, Inc.
Cover design by Rose Audette
Cover and interior illustrations © Alece Birnbach

Sourcebooks and the colophon are registered trademarks of Sourcebooks, Inc.

The characters and events portrayed in this book are fictitious or are used ficti-
tiously. Any similarity to real persons, living or dead, is purely coincidental and
not intended by the author.

Published by Sourcebooks Jabberwocky, an imprint of Sourcebooks, Inc.
P.O. Box 4410, Naperville, Illinois 60567-4410
(630) 961-3900
Fax: (630) 961-2168
www.jabberwockykids.com

Library of Congress Cataloging-in-Publication data is on file with the pub-
lisher.

Source of Production: Versa Press, East Peoria, Illinois, USA
Date of Production: May 2014
Run Number: 5001600

Printed and bound in the United States of America.
VP 10 9 8 7 6 5 4 3 2 1

Dorothy's Derby Chronicles

Rise of the Undead Redhead

Written by Meghan Dougherty with Karen Windness

Illustrated by Alece Birnbach

sourcebooks
jabberwocky

Chapter 1

Dorothy and Samantha let out terrified shrieks as Grandma Sally gunned the engine, catapulting the hearse over a speed bump and into the school parking lot.

"Are you trying to kill us?" Dorothy squealed.

"Seriously, girls," Grandma said, touching up her orange lipstick in the rearview mirror while steering with one elbow. "You both act like you've never been in a car before."

"Watch out!" Sam screamed, pressing her feet into the back of her older sister's seat. Dorothy looked to the backseat at Sam, who mimed "crazy" by circling her ear with her finger, half smiling.

Grandma swerved just in time to miss a pair of teachers who sprang out of the way, paperwork and books flying.

"Get out of the road, nerds!" Grandma yelled as she tucked the capped tube of lipstick back into her bra.

Grandma's little dog chimed in with a *Yap! Yap! Yap!* through the curtains of the rear window.

"That's right, Morti," Grandma said. "You tell 'em."

"Look, Grandma. There's a spot," Dorothy suggested hopefully. It was a shady space in the back corner of the small parking lot.

"No chance, Dot. Nothing but valet service for Dead Betty," Grandma said, patting the checkered dashboard.

Figures, Dorothy thought. *No one ever listens to me.* She screwed her eyes shut. *Maybe we'll all die before we get to the entrance.* That would teach Mom not to dump them with their nutcase grandma clear across the country.

The car screeched to a whiplash stop right in front of J. Elway Middle School and Grandma pinched Dorothy's arm. "Wake up, chicky. We're here."

Rats. Still alive.

"You can't park here," Sam said, pointing to the large NO PARKING sign looming above the hearse.

Grandma reached into the backseat for her leopard-print purse. "Dorothy and I will only be a minute, hon."

"Um…really, Grandma," Dorothy stammered. "I'm almost twelve years old. I can go by myself."

But it was too late. Grandma was already out of the car, yelling like a peanut vendor at a baseball game, "What you lookin' at?" and, "Take a picture. It lasts longer," to the students filing out of the school bus that had just parked behind them.

Grandma knocked at the window with a ruby-eyed skull ring, her shiny black suit reflecting Dorothy's frizzy red hair through the glass. "Dorothy Moore! Quit fartin' around and come meet your new friends," she ordered, gesturing to the kids she'd just yelled at.

"Please, Grandma." Dorothy's heart was racing. "Let's just go back to the funeral home." She had been living in an old mortuary since Monday, and the last two days hadn't made Grandma's house any less creepy. Still, Dorothy would rather hang out with corpses any day than face the crowd that had formed around the hearse.

Grandma made a disappointed clucking sound with her tongue and swung the car door open. A chilly September breeze swept over Dorothy's bare, freckled legs. She gazed out at the sea of shocked and amused faces and realized she'd made another huge mistake. That morning, Grandma had said it would be "groovy" if Dorothy wore the uniform from her old school, a long-sleeved blouse and plaid skirt—at least until they could buy a new one with the money Mom had promised to send soon.

But these kids weren't wearing uniforms. They were dressed in jeans, classic rock T-shirts with hoodies, cute cardigans with matching boots. Dorothy stared down at her pleated plaid skirt, yellowing button-up blouse, and clunky black shoes.

Grandma tapped her fake nails impatiently on the roof of the car. "Look alive, Dorth."

Okay. I can do this, Dorothy thought. She swung her backpack up onto her shoulder and stepped out of the hearse. But her left foot caught on the car's door frame and she fell forward, both knees scraping painfully on the sidewalk. Cackles and delighted hoots erupted from the crowd. "Frappit!" Dorothy cursed. *So much for first impressions*, she thought, finding her feet and giving the onlookers a little wave and an awkward smile.

"Atta girl!" Grandma said, slapping Dorothy on the rump.

Grandma led the way to the stately front entrance, all the way clickety-clacking on high heels the same hot pink color as her short, spiky hair.

"Why can't I have a normal grandma?" Dorothy grumbled.

Grandma laughed. "Normal is overrated."

Dorothy glanced back at the car. Morti was now in the front passenger seat licking the inside of the window. From the backseat, Sam shook her strawberry-colored pigtails and smirked devilishly at Dorothy through the tinted glass.

"You're next," Dorothy mouthed. McNeil Elementary was only a couple of blocks away. Sam mimed back, open mouthed, "Nooo!" with her hands on her cheeks, shaking her head vigorously.

The gawking mob had grown, and Grandma began waving like she was the float queen in a two-person parade. "Friendly folks," she said, pushing open the heavy front door. "I think you're going to like this school."

Dorothy could already hear the jokes spreading. Kids were whispering things like, "Crazy Granny drives a cursed hearse," and "Watch out for falling redheads!"

As she stepped into J. Elway Middle School, the doors to Dorothy's own living nightmare banged shut behind her.

Chapter 2

"I am the unluckiest person on the planet," Dorothy muttered.

Locker #13 just stared back at her with six pairs of adorable unblinking eyes. The door was decorated with sparkly stickers: a seahorse in an evening gown, a unicorn blowing heart-shaped bubbles, an otter dripping with jewels, a lollipop licking its own eye, a centipede in high heels, and a penguin wearing a "Mr. Pretty" sash. And all of them seemed to be saying, "Sorry! Too busy being cute to care!"

Dorothy dumped her backpack to the ground and looked down again at the handful of admission paperwork. She reentered the locker combination, and the latch made a clicking sound, but the door wouldn't open.

Rats! No wonder this thing is available!

"Yo, Hearse Girl!"

"Eyaaack!" Dorothy screeched, tossing her papers everywhere at the loud, whispering, baritone voice at her ear. She whirled around and got a face full of curly brown hair in the process.

"Watch the fro," exclaimed a girl in a denim jacket. Her skin was the color of milk chocolate. "My hair isn't cotton candy, you know."

Dorothy fell backward and gasped for air.

The girl propped her fists on curvy hips that looked out of place on her otherwise skinny body. "I didn't scare you, did I, Hearse Girl?"

Dorothy shook her head. "No. That's okay. I was, um, actually just getting ready to scream and throw my papers into the air."

The girl laughed. "You're funny, Hearse Girl. I'm Gigi Johnston. And you're Dorothy Moore, right?"

Dorothy frowned. "You knew my name and still called me Hearse Girl?"

"Just messin' around," Gigi said. "Here, I'll make it up to you." She gave Dorothy's locker a solid punch right next to the combination dial. The door made a popping sound and opened.

"Wow. Thanks!" Dorothy peered inside the locker. She was greeted by a large, lip-shaped sticker that said, "Hugs 'n' Kisses!"

"Excuse me," said a soft voice. Dorothy turned to see a petite Asian girl appearing from behind Gigi's halo of brown curls. She was clad entirely in black and looked like a girly ninja, except for the combat boots and pink highlights in her hair. "I think these are yours," she said, handing Dorothy her paperwork arranged in a neat little pile.

Gigi bumped the girl with her hip. "So, you going to ask her, or should I?"

"Shut it," the girl whispered, returning a bump so

forceful that Gigi lost her footing for a moment. "I told you I'd ask her myself."

Gigi snorted. "Whatever, Jade. I got her for you, didn't I?"

"Hey. Ask me what?" Dorothy said.

Jade blew a strand of hair out of her eyes and looked casually back over both shoulders. "It's about the hearse," she began mysteriously. "It's just...I'm *dying* to know. Was there a corpse in there?"

Dorothy felt the hairs on the back of her neck rise. "No, not this morning there wasn't. But my grandma did say she was giving Uncle Dirt Nap a ride later today."

"Who's Uncle Dirt Nap?" Gigi asked.

"It's a nickname for a dead person," Jade said, a childlike grin spread across her heart-shaped face. "It *is* a real hearse."

Gigi shrugged. "All righty, Goth Girl. Now you know. Time to get to class."

"Oh, right. Me, too," Dorothy said, suddenly feeling self-conscious. She shoved the stack of papers from her backpack into her locker and shut the door—right on her fingers. "Ow! Ow! Ow!" Dorothy yelped, trying to pull her hand free.

In a flash, Gigi grabbed the bottom corner of the locker door and pried it open as Jade removed Dorothy's trapped hand, one finger at a time.

"Th-thank you," Dorothy stuttered, caressing her throbbing fingers. Her throat stung and she willed herself not to cry, but tears began to tumble down her cheeks anyway.

"Oh, honey," Gigi cooed, folding Dorothy into her arms. "You poor thing."

Dorothy couldn't believe she was crying now. She could have cried a million times during the move, but she hadn't. Not once. She had to be strong for Sam now that Mom wasn't around. But here Dorothy was, sobbing into the jean lapel of some crazy-haired girl she had just met.

"Oh, dear," Jade said. "How bad are your fingers?"

Dorothy wiped her eyes and held out her hand.

"Uh-oh," Gigi said, turning the hand over in hers. "Looks like you'll be the next person getting a ride in the back of that hearse."

Dorothy laughed through her tears. "Just pinched, I think."

A warning bell rang.

"What's your first class?" Jade asked.

Dorothy snuffled. "Gym."

"Seriously?" Gigi said. "Did you break a mirror or walk under a ladder or something?"

Jade waved Gigi away. "Just ignore her. You'll be fine. I have homeroom gym, too. Ms. Nailer's class. You can go with me, if you want. I still have to put on my tattoos before class starts."

Tattoos? Dorothy wondered.

"Give the Pompoms a smooch from me," Gigi said, popping in a pair of earphones. She flashed the peace sign and then cranked up the volume on her player— loud enough that Dorothy could feel the reggae bass line pulsating in her teeth. Gigi bounced, jiggled, and shimmied her way over to a line of lockers a few rows away.

"Who are the Pompoms?" Dorothy asked, gingerly pulling her backpack over one shoulder. Her fingers were still throbbing.

"They're just a club of pretty, blond, popular girls," Jade said, merging into the hallway traffic with Dorothy trailing behind.

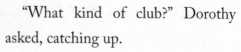

"What kind of club?" Dorothy asked, catching up.

"Pompoms Cheer for a Better Planet!" Jade said in an animated, high-pitched voice. Then, her voice turning sour, "But it's all a bunch of crap, if you ask me."

JADE'S TATS

Jade weaved smoothly through a pack of chattering students. Dorothy tripped and bumped her way through the same group and was elbowed and yelled at more than once.

The hallway became less crowded as they passed a cafeteria that already smelled like burnt meatloaf.

"You see that organic garden?" Jade asked, pointing through a picture window. It looked out onto a small plot of ground with rows of cornstalks and tomato plants and other leafy greens Dorothy didn't recognize.

"The Pompoms did that?" Dorothy asked, impressed.

"Nope. Gigi and I planted that garden. We asked the Pompoms to help, but they said they were too busy chopping down trees for the Save-the-Forest Bonfire."

Dorothy gasped. "But that's like killing trees to save trees."

Jade nodded her head. "That's what I said."

Dorothy and Jade walked a few more minutes in silence and then stopped in front of a door that read Girls' Locker Room.

"Something else before you meet the Pompoms," Jade said. "Whatever you do, be sure to avoid Alex. She's the snobbiest and prettiest Pompom and loves to target the mutants who bring the school down, like me and Gigi." Jade pushed her shoulder against the door. "She'll hate you, too, of course."

Dorothy raised an eyebrow. "You're calling *me* a mutant?"

"Oh, I'm sorry," Jade said sarcastically as she held the door open for Dorothy. "I guess it must be normal where you come from to ride around in a hearse and wear a kilt to school."

Dorothy sighed. "Okay. I guess you have a point."

As Dorothy stepped into the locker room, she took some comfort knowing that in a few short minutes she would be wearing her navy gym shorts, white T-shirt, and worn Converse sneakers. It would be nice to be dressed in something normal for at least one class that day—even if she was starting to think that the weirdos at this school might be good company.

DODGEBALL!

Chapter 3

Once she'd changed, Dorothy trudged after Jade into the brightly lit gymnasium. The room was abuzz with girls giggling and talking, which fortunately drowned out the high-pitched squeaks Dorothy's shoes made on the shiny linoleum.

"So much for wearing something normal," Dorothy grumbled, looking down at the sparkly tiger-striped jumpsuit she had found in her backpack. Her regular gym clothes had disappeared, replaced with the jumpsuit and a note that read, "Don't say I never gave you anything. Love, Grandma."

"I think it's kind of cool," Jade said.

"Really?" The outfit looked like something Dorothy had seen an aerobics instructor wear on a TV show called "Groovin' with the Geezers."

"Sure," Jade said with a smirk. "You look... GRRRrrreat!"

Dorothy groaned.

Jade came to a sudden stop. "The Pompoms are at it again," she said, nodding in the direction of two pretty girls in cheerleader outfits, each with a blond ponytail sticking out of the top of her head like a tree. One of them had dazzling white teeth and the other had shiny, lip-glossed lips. They were throwing a book over the head of a very tall girl with braces and thick glasses.

"Give me back my Space Fleet manual!" the tall girl pleaded, waving her skinny arms awkwardly above her head.

"No way, geek!" the lip gloss Pompom said, lobbing the book back to her grinning friend.

"As an official Federation Science Officer, I order you to return my manual!" the geek shouted desperately.

"Or what? You're going to zap us with your photon torpedoes?" Both Pompoms laughed devilishly.

"Wait here," Jade said. She crouched and approached the Pompoms, silently springing up, intercepting the book as it sailed through the air. Jade placed the manual into the geek's shaking hands and strolled calmly back to Dorothy.

Wow. Nice move, Dorothy thought.

"You're a good Earthling, Jade," the geek called, holding the manual to her chest as she skittered away.

"And a dead one," the Pompom giggled.

"Hold up," the other girl said, grabbing her friend's arm as she caught sight of Dorothy. There was something in how she smacked her shiny lips together that made Dorothy think of hungry lions during feeding time at the zoo. "Alexandra is going to flip out when she sees this!"

The other Pompom bared her dazzling, white teeth. "Hey, Alex!" she shouted to a group of girls with the same treetop hairdos. They were all blond and beautiful and impossible to tell apart.

"Lovely," Jade groaned. "Whatever happens, just stay behind me, okay, Dorothy?"

Dorothy's hands began to tremble and her tongue felt like it had turned into cotton. From over Jade's head, she watched a gorgeous girl emerge from the group of Pompoms, toss a silky blond ponytail over her shoulder, and walk in their direction. The tree-haired girls followed like a pack of obedient puppy dogs.

"You called?" the gorgeous girl said while casually zipping up a pink velour jacket.

Jade pushed up her sleeves to reveal slender arms covered with several menacing temporary tattoos. "Just back off, Alex."

The lip gloss Pompom pointed at Dorothy. "Check out Jade's new freak!"

Dorothy cowered behind her petite friend, but Alex had already targeted her with ice blue, laser beam eyes.

"Her name is Dorothy, and she is not a freak," Jade snarled.

They're going to eat us alive, Dorothy thought, surveying the group of girls that surrounded them.

Dorothy forced herself to smile and stepped out from behind Jade. She wiped her sweaty hand on her outfit and presented it to Alex. "Um, hi! Nice to meet you."

Alex gasped as she got the full effect of Dorothy's gym outfit. "What are you wearing? Are those…sequins?"

Dorothy's courage shrank like a wool sweater in the dryer. She withdrew her hand and opened her mouth to say something, but nothing came out. She was wearing sequins. The tiger-striped outfit was covered in them.

Alex took several steps backward, staring at Dorothy as if she might catch a terrible sequin disease if she stood too close.

One of the tree-haired Pompoms tittered and said, "Did your crazy granny dress you?"

Dorothy bit her bottom lip and shrugged. *Grandma Sally strikes again.*

"Are you wearing her underpants, too?" another girl

teased. The Pompoms roared with laughter, except for Alex, who raised a manicured hand to cover her face. Dorothy tugged self-consciously at the back of her sparkly jumpsuit.

"You can't make fun of her!" Jade hissed. "Not while you're wearing those stupid ponytails. What are they supposed to be, anyway? Nuclear mushroom clouds for some awareness project?"

"Nuh-uh, Jade," one of the girls said. "Bombs Are a Bummer Day isn't until next week!"

"Right," agreed another Pompom, fluffing the top of her ponytail. "These are whale spouts. They remind everyone of how adorable whales are."

"Adorable?" Jade exclaimed. "What ever happened to saving the whales?"

A whistle blew, and all the girls turned to see a muscular woman with a buzz cut and camouflage shorts marching their way. "Having a problem, are we?" the gym teacher said, her single black eyebrow making a V in the middle of her forehead.

"Great," Jade mumbled. "Ms. Nailer."

Phew! We're saved! Dorothy thought.

"Why don't we resolve this problem the sportsman-like way, shall we?" the gym teacher said, a gleam in her dark, beady eyes.

"Dodgeball!" the Pompoms cheered.

Not dodgeball, Dorothy thought. *Why can't it be something I'm good at, like beanbag toss or the parachute game?*

"How about you give us an automatic A if we send the new girl to the nurse's office," the lip gloss Pompom said cheerily.

"You will get yourself into a heap of trouble with that kind of talk, missy," Ms. Nailer said to lip gloss, smiling at Dorothy with yellow, sharp-looking teeth. "But, in about five seconds this new recruit will see that I demand my soldiers give me an aggressive, 110 stinging percent."

Ms. Nailer gave one of the Pompoms the first pick, and teams ended up with Pompoms on one side and everybody else on the other. Ms. Nailer arranged red rubber balls down the center of the basketball court as Dorothy surveyed the collection of misfits on her side of the line. Besides Dorothy and Jade, there was a big girl with rosy cheeks who giggled like a nervous hyena; a short, hyperactive girl who jumped around like there were fire ants colonizing in her gym socks; a girl with chestnut skin and long jet-black hair that fell into her eyes, staring at the floor; and the tall Star Fleet geek, who still clutched her manual like a security blanket.

"We're dead," Dorothy whispered to Jade.

"Speak for yourself," Jade said, crouching into a ready stance.

Ms. Nailer blew her whistle, launching the Pompoms into attack mode.

"Nobody touch the new girl!" the lip gloss Pompom yelled as she and her teammates rushed to the line of balls. Dorothy couldn't believe her ears. Did the Pompoms feel bad for her after all? The girl scampered back to Alex and handed her a ball saying, "Dorothy is all yours." Dorothy gulped and skittered to the back of the court.

"Pssst…You're going down, Thunder Thighs," a Pompom growled lowly as she pitched her ball at the big girl's feet. The girl sprang into the air, but instead of jumping over the ball, she landed on top of it. Her arms flailed, and she shuffled her feet backward as the ball whisked her right into the Pompoms' court. Dorothy was astounded by the girl's raw power as she unwittingly steamrolled the Pompom who had thrown the ball. Like a bulldozer, she uprooted three other tree-haired Pompoms before she finally crashed into a support beam at the far end of the gym.

"Oh, gosh! My bad! My bad!" the girl apologized, and went into a fit of nervous giggles.

"Off the floor, Ruth," Ms. Nailer ordered.

The Pompoms regrouped, and one of them yelled, "The geek is next!" A ball rocketed toward the Star Fleet nerd.

"That's enough," Ms. Nailer said, with her lips curled into a hint of a smirk.

Dorothy held her breath, but to her surprise the tall girl didn't flinch. Calmly, she took a calculated step to the right and extended her manual to the left. The ball smashed into the book and returned to the Pompom who had just thrown it like a heat-seeking missile.

The ball smacked the top of the Pompom's head,

smashing her whale spout hairdo. "No fair, Lizzy!" she shrieked.

"Brains over brawn," Lizzy said, pushing her eyeglasses up her nose in satisfaction.

"Heads up!" Ms. Nailer shouted near Alexandra just as Jade let her ball fly. Alex twirled out of the way with the grace of a dancer and then tossed her ball in a pretty arc toward Jade. Jade somersaulted forward, landed in a crouching stance, and then vanished like smoke between Lizzy and the hyperactive girl.

The energetic girl clapped her hands like a windup monkey. "Wow, that was supercool!" she said. "First Alex was like…" she spun in a circle, "and then Jade was like…" the girl launched herself into a flying somersault, and landed with an "oof!" on her back.

"Dinah's down!" Ms. Nailer yelled. Dinah struggled to pull air into her lungs as the Pompoms pummeled her with every ball they had.

"Stop it! Stop it now!" Jade yelled. "Are you okay, Dinah?" she said, helping the twitching girl to her feet.

"Oh, yeah. Yeah, totally," Dinah wheezed, shaking herself off. "Hey, did you see me flip? First I was like…"

Ms. Nailer blew her whistle. "You're out, Dinah."

Dinah skipped happily off the floor, reminding Dorothy of her seven-year-old sister.

I hope Sam's having a better day than I am, Dorothy thought as she looked around for somewhere safe to hide.

The shy, dark-haired girl was standing alone in the back corner of the gym floor. She was so quiet and still that she almost disappeared into her surroundings.

The Pompoms will never find me there, Dorothy thought as she made her way over to the girl.

The shy girl peeked out through the curtains of black hair that framed her face. "What is you doing?" she whispered in a heavy Spanish accent.

"Oh, nothing," Dorothy said innocently as she tip-toed behind the girl.

"Dorothy's behind Juana!" a Pompom shouted, zing-ing a ball toward the dark-haired girl.

With the reflexes of a panther, Juana snatched the ball out of the air. She swiveled and pressed the ball firmly into Dorothy's sequined chest. "Leesten, Dorty. You needs to be brave."

Dorothy gulped. "Brave?"

"Trust me. Dey will picks on you until you show your...strongness, no?"

Dorothy sighed and accepted the ball reluctantly. Juana was right. Alex and the Pompoms weren't going to stop hunting her—unless she found a way to make them stop.

Dorothy scanned the playing floor. Jade's pace had slowed to a jog as she launched balls at Alex like a tennis ball machine. Alex leapt and spun gracefully out of the way of Jade's attacks.

If Jade is so tired, why doesn't she pass some balls to her teammates? Dorothy wondered.

When Jade finally ran out of ammo, Alex bent over to pick up a ball of her own.

Juana gave Dorothy a thumbs-up. *Now or never,* Dorothy thought, her heart thundering in her chest. She took aim at Alex, closed her eyes, and threw the ball with all her strength.

Dorothy heard cheering, shouting, and laughter. She opened her eyes...just in time to take a face full of hard rubber ball. Her face stung, her ears buzzed, and she tasted something like pennies in her mouth. She reached up to touch her throbbing nose and felt something wet. Her head swam. She felt her knees buckle and the world suddenly went black.

Chapter 4

Dorothy opened her eyes to a brilliant white light. "I…
died?" she wondered aloud.

"And went to heaven!" Gigi teased, flipping off an
overhead lamp.

"Where am I?" Dorothy wondered. She wasn't in the
gymnasium. She was lying on a hard bed in a small room
decorated with framed photos of kids wearing casts and
leaning on crutches.

"The nurse's office, silly," Jade said, appearing beside
the bed.

"How's my patient feeling?" Gigi asked.

"Dizzy," Dorothy said. "Wait. You're the nurse?" Gigi

was nice enough, but she seemed better suited for croco-dile wrestling than nursing.

"Nurse Boils is in the gym helping some Pompoms," Jade said. "She told me I could get Gigi for you."

"I'm first aid certified!" Gigi said proudly.

The nurse is helping Pompoms? "Oh crap. Did I hit Alex as hard as she hit me? She's okay, right?"

Both Gigi and Jade laughed.

"No, Alex is just fine," Jade said. "You didn't hit her. You hit the basketball hoop. The ball bounced back into your face."

"You mean I sent *myself* to the nurse's office?" Dorothy moaned and covered her eyes with her hand.

Gigi peeled Dorothy's hand away and popped a stethoscope on her patient's forehead. "Your nose isn't broken, and you don't have a concussion, but I can't figure out why you passed out."

"Blood," Dorothy said, her stomach twisting. "It makes me faint. Hey, I earned that A, though, right? You know, for sending myself to the nurse's office?"

"Uh, sure," Jade said, not sounding sure at all.

"Guess what else you earned?" Gigi said. "A trip home! Nurse Boils called your grandma. She's coming to pick you up."

Dorothy gulped. "Grandma? Picking me up?" Her hands started to shake again. After all she had gone through that morning, another ride in Dead Betty would probably kill her. Just thinking about it made Dorothy's heart thump against her rib cage and her breath come out in short, panicky bursts.

"She's going into cardiac arrest!" Gigi shouted. In a flash, Gigi was on top of the bed, straddling Dorothy's belly and pressing her hands hard into her patient's chest. Now Dorothy *really* couldn't breathe.

"She's turning blue, Gigi! Do something," Jade yelped.

"I'm trying!" Gigi said, now beating on Dorothy's ribs with her fists.

Desperate to free herself, Dorothy rolled hard onto her left side. Gigi flailed and toppled to the ground, dragging Dorothy down with her.

"Get off me," Gigi groaned. But Dorothy felt paralyzed. All the wind had been knocked out of her lungs.

Like a weightlifter, Gigi heaved Dorothy onto the cold linoleum floor.

"It worked," Jade cheered. "Look. She's breathing again." Jade knelt next to Dorothy. "You okay?"

Dorothy sputtered out a weak, "Uh-huh." But her nose started to tingle. It was probably going to bleed again. And why was the ceiling spinning? She felt her body float gently upward, and she realized vaguely that she was being lifted back onto the bed.

Gigi shook her head. "We can't let her go home alone like this. She's a mess!"

A mischievous grin tugged at the corners of Jade's lips. "That's a shame," she said. "I guess we'll just have to go home with her."

What is it with Jade and Grandma's hearse? Dorothy thought lazily. But she returned Jade's grin with a goofy smile anyway. *Friends! At my house!*

Nurse Boils showed up a short while later to check on Dorothy. The nurse was a plump, pink-faced woman with auburn hair, sparkly green eyes, and a gap between her two front teeth.

"That was quite the dodgeball game," the nurse said cheerily. "Several bruises, four broken fingernails, and we even had a fainter."

Dorothy blushed.

"You ready to go home, deary?" Nurse Boils asked, smoothing Dorothy's hair. "Your ride is here."

"I guess so," Dorothy said, trying to sit up. She still felt dizzy, though, and slumped back onto the bed.

Nurse Boils clicked her tongue and pulled a white bedsheet up under Dorothy's chin. "Well then. I suppose Jade and Gigi will just have to wheel you out."

"In a wheelchair?" Dorothy asked, already feeling embarrassed.

Jade shook her head. "Gurney. That bed you're lying on rolls."

Dorothy groaned.

"Oh, come on!" Gigi said. "It'll be fun. Plus, I always wanted to give someone a ride on this thing."

Nurse Boils unlocked the bed wheels, and Jade and Gigi pushed the gurney into the hall.

They were nearly to the exit when a bell rang and a sea

of noisy students flooded the hallway. *Frappit,* Dorothy thought, yanking the white sheet over her head. The yelling and chattering stopped suddenly.

"Who's under the sheet?" a boy asked, his voice cracking mid-sentence.

"The new girl. Death by dodgeball, you know," Gigi said in an official tone that would have won her a role as a TV doctor. "Very tragic."

Dorothy heard gasps and muffled shrieks. She suppressed the urge to giggle and tried to lie as still as possible. Actually, this being dead thing was kind of fun.

Once the gurney was outside, Dorothy heard Grandma yell, "Hey! Did someone call for a hearse?"

Grandma's face appeared under the sheet. "So you're dead, eh?"

"Just a little," Dorothy said, pushing herself up on her elbows.

"You just sit tight, hon. The nurse told me you have the spins. We're going to put you in the back."

"The back? Uncle Dirt Nap's not in there, is he?"

"Now don't you worry, Dot," Grandma said with a

wink. "There's plenty of room for more than one dead body in back."

Dorothy bolted straight up. Her nose started to flow again, soaking the sheet with blood. The last thing she heard before she passed out was the sound of students screaming in the distance.

In the blackness, Dorothy dreamt she was on a moon-lit racetrack. Her feet had transformed into wheels and adrenaline revved through her veins like gasoline. A gun-shot shattered the still of the stadium, and Dorothy flew into action, racing around the oval track like a precision sports car. After what seemed like a hundred laps, other machine girls appeared on the track ahead of her. As Dorothy flew toward them, she noticed that they were wearing tattered cheerleader uniforms. Bones peeked out through their gray-green skin, and their moans vibrated inside Dorothy's head. Terrified, Dorothy tried to slow down, but she didn't have any brakes. She barreled headlong through the pack of dead girls as pieces of their shredded, slimy uniforms flapped against her face.

Dorothy's eyes flew open. Morti, who had been

licking her cheeks, yipped happily as she sat up. She was back in her bedroom at the funeral home.

"Hello, sunshine," Jade said, putting down a sketch-book and pencil.

"About time!" Gigi added. "You were out forever. I was beginning to think you were in a coma or something."

"I was just…really tired," Dorothy said, realizing that she hadn't had a decent night's sleep in days. She stretched her arms and yawned. Despite the freaky dream, she actually felt a lot better.

"What time is it?" Dorothy asked.

Jade plucked the cell phone off Dorothy's nightstand and showed it to her. "Almost two o'clock," Dorothy said. *And no new messages from Mom,* she thought to herself.

"Your grandma's off doing mortuary stuff," Gigi said. "But she says she's sorry about the Uncle Dirt Nap joke."

"You mean there wasn't a dead person in the back of the hearse?"

"Just you," Jade said with an impish grin.

"She said she'd take us to Galactic Skate later. If you're feeling up to it," Gigi said.

"What's Galactic Skate?" Dorothy asked, scratching Morti behind his pointy ears.

"An old roller rink," Jade explained.

Dorothy stopped scratching. "Like, for roller-skating?" Her heart skipped a beat. Her mom had forbidden her from ever roller-skating.

"And pizza," Gigi said. "I could go for a slice of their pepperoni right now. Hot and greasy."

"Eww," Jade said, making a face.

"Hey, just because you don't eat pepperoni doesn't mean I can't enjoy it."

Jade sighed. "Whatever, meat eater." She turned to Dorothy. "I hope it's okay, but we gave your uniform a makeover while you were sleeping."

"Wait. You what?" Dorothy's mind had been wandering. She was remembering how she had not been allowed to go to her best friend's tenth birthday party— just because it was at Skate Land.

Her mom had said, "If God wanted us to roller-skate, He would have given us wheels instead of feet."

Just like my dream, Dorothy thought with a shiver.

"Your outfit. We're fixing it. It's almost done and close to cool now, see?" Gigi said, holding up a pink blouse and a short, pink plaid skirt. "Jade came up with the design and did all the sewing and stuff, but I helped with the dye. It's still pretty wet." The bottom of her skirt had been transformed into a killer scarf and belt.

"That's my uniform?" Dorothy said, sitting up to get a better look. She felt so happy she could cry. "It's amazing!"

Jade blushed and looked out Dorothy's bedroom door. "Hey, your house is cool," she said. "You didn't tell us you lived *in* the funeral home."

"Just moved in," Dorothy said, swinging her legs over the side of the bed. "The top floors of the mortuary aren't used anymore, but it's still creepy. Grandma's a retired mortician, so she's collected some weird stuff."

"Like that?" Jade was pointing at the wardrobe closet standing in the corner of Dorothy's small room. It was made from two coffins joined together.

Dorothy nodded and bit her lip.

The dark wood and satin lining was pretty, but it gave her nightmares. Last night she'd dreamt that Dracula and his wife were living inside the closet. The vampire couple had spent the whole dream arguing about whether they should drink all of Dorothy's blood in one sitting or drain her slowly night after night.

"But if your grandma's retired, why's she working for the funeral home?" Gigi asked.

"Oh," Dorothy said. "Well, she still owns the place, and she likes to work part time. Plus, they say nobody can fill in a bullet hole like Grandma."

"Nice," Jade said darkly.

"Oh sure, I can't eat pepperoni, but you get all giddy over dead people and bullet holes and stuff," Gigi said.

"It is not the same thing," Jade argued.

"So," Dorothy said, changing the subject. "You guys want the tour?"

Dorothy escorted her new friends around the three-story Victorian house. From outside it looked like a haunted house, minus the broken windows, cobwebs, and ghosts. At least Dorothy hoped there weren't any ghosts. The mortuary had an excellent view of Prospect Cemetery. The bottom floors of the building were a working funeral home, and the top two floors were Grandma's house. They had been converted into living quarters when Grandma retired and sold the business to a young couple just out of mortuary school.

Other than adding a separate entrance, Grandma hadn't made many renovations. It was still every bit a funeral parlor. Instead of buying new furniture, Grandma "got her craft on" and turned the old funeral gear into furniture and decorations. Mortuary couture, she called it. You hardly knew the top floors weren't a working funeral home. There were flower arrangements everywhere, rolling gurneys for couches, and an embalming table for a dining room table, complete with church kneelers instead of chairs. Grandma said it was good for the core, but bad on the knees. Religious symbols dotted the walls, too, although Grandma had never been the churchgoing type.

Grandma slept in Slumber Room Number 1 (at least that's what the plaque on the door said), and Dorothy's and Sam's rooms were in the attic. There weren't any plaques on their bedroom doors, which was just fine by Dorothy. Because Grandma still worked at the funeral home they had the run of the place, although Dorothy was too spooked to wander much. The fewer details she knew, the better. The whole place gave her the willies.

"Home sweet home!" Dorothy said when the tour was over. *At least until Mom comes back. If she comes back.*

Chapter 5

By the time Grandma and Sam arrived home, Dorothy, Gigi, and Jade had shared a bag of chips and watched three episodes of *Cupcake Smackdown* on the Food Channel. Dorothy's outfit was finally dry, so she quickly changed out of her bloodstained jumper and they all piled into Grandma's hearse. Gigi estimated a fifteen-minute drive to Galactic Skate, but it couldn't have been more than six minutes before they were pulling into the parking lot. Still plenty of time for Dorothy to check her cell phone a hundred times for messages from Mom. It would be like Mom to not check in for days and then call right as they were going roller-skating.

"Earth to Dorothy!" Grandma was standing at the Galactic Skate entrance, a leopard-print duffel bag hitched over her shoulder. Gigi, Jade, and Sam had to have already gone inside. Dorothy blinked. After exiting the car, she had been mesmerized by the huge mural on the side of the large, square building. Three disco-era roller skaters whooshed across the brick wall: a fist-pumping woman with a huge red afro, a tall woman with dark skin and bobbed pigtails, and a thin Asian woman with long hair that rippled behind her like a black flag.

"Coming!" Dorothy called. *I can't believe I'm going roller-skating. Mom's going to kill me!*

They bought skate passes from a fat, balding man with a thick salt-and-pepper mustache and then walked toward the food court area. The inside of Galactic Skate was dimly lit and stank like old french fries. Dusty ceiling fans spun around at awkward angles, and the star-patterned carpet felt sticky under Dorothy's feet. Near the entrance there was a tiny concession area with tables, chairs, and a few video games with out-of-order signs taped to the screens. Farther in was a large wood-floor rink surrounded by a waist-high wood partition covered in the same dingy carpeting. A narrow skate changing area was positioned at the entrance to the rink. Dorothy could see a couple of teenagers exiting the skate floor through a gap in the wall, but otherwise the place was empty.

"I'm hungry!" Gigi said as they passed by an unmanned concession cart where two flies danced on a half-eaten hot dog.

"I don't know about this," Dorothy said. "Galactic Skate is, um…"

Jade coughed something that sounded like "armpit?" and pulled a bottle of hand sanitizer out of her messenger bag. She pumped several squirts into her already clean hands.

"Girls!" Grandma scolded. "Galactic Skate is like a second home to me. This is where I met the love of my life," she added nostalgically.

Sam squealed with delight. "Our grandfather?"

Grandma chuckled. "No, Sam. Well yes, I did meet your grandpa here, but I'm talking about this." Grandma pulled a pair of black, sneaker-style roller skates out of her bag and kissed them on the laces. The black leather was clean but creased with age and use, like an old Harley jacket that had seen plenty of adventure.

Jade gagged audibly, but Dorothy's fingers itched to touch the forbidden skates.

"Enough memory lane, G-ma," Gigi said. "It's skate time."

Dorothy's heart thumped against the cell phone now tucked inside her shirt. The time had come to break Mom's number one rule: No roller-skating. Ever.

Sam cartwheeled. "Hooray for roller-skating!" she cheered.

Dorothy sighed. *I don't get it. Sam isn't worried, she's excited. Why am I such a chicken?*

"Brown bombers over there," Grandma said, pointing to a wall of bookshelves filled with worn leather skates. A rocket-shaped rental desk sat next to the shelves, and an old man dozed behind it, snoring loudly. His skin was as wrinkled as the weathered skates.

Gigi, Jade, and Sam raced to the desk, but Dorothy's feet felt like anchors. Was she really capable of betraying her mom like this?

"Hey, Dot," Grandma said. "Why don't you come with me instead?"

Dorothy breathed a sigh of relief. Maybe she wouldn't have to skate, after all. She had passed out at school today, right?

Grandma led Dorothy to a corner booth. "You know," Grandma said, placing her black skates on the table after they had sat down. "I always wanted to give these babies to your mom."

Dorothy eyed the skates longingly. "But Mom hates roller-skating."

Grandma nodded. "And that's why she can never know about this." Grandma winked and rolled the skates over to Dorothy.

Dorothy's jaw fell open and she caught the skates in her open hands. The leather was worn but supple. "For me?" A bolt of rebellious excitement flashed through her body. "You *really* want me to have them?"

"Yep. All yours," Grandma said. "And I bet they'll fit you, too. I was about your age when I started skating."

Dorothy swung her feet to the side of the bench and kicked off her clunky black shoes. With skates like these, who cared what Mom thought?

A boy with olive skin, dark curly hair, and a dimpled chin skated up to their booth. He was wearing silver roller blades, dark blue jeans, and a long-sleeved T-shirt. He looked a couple of years older than Dorothy. He tapped Grandma on the shoulder.

"Max, my boyfriend," Grandma said. She stood up and exchanged a complicated handshake that involved a shoulder bump, several hand slaps, and a move that looked like a zombie doing the robot dance.

"Don't tell me you're skipping ladies' night to come to Galactic Skate," Max said.

"Let's just call this little ladies' night," Grandma said, nodding to Dorothy. "This is my granddaughter."

Max glanced over at Dorothy, who had managed to get herself into an unladylike position while pulling on her new skates.

"Um, hi. I'm Dorothy," she said, looking up from a tangle of laces.

Max nodded and gave Dorothy a lopsided grin.

He's smiling at me, Dorothy thought. *A cute boy, smiling at me. Wait, can he see my underwear? Frappit! My short skirt! I'm such an idiot.*

Dorothy quickly crossed her ankles. But with her laces still tangled, she lost her balance and tumbled forward off the bench. Max leapt to Dorothy's rescue, catching her mid-fall before returning her to her seat.

"Uh, thanks," Dorothy said, her cheeks hot.

Max politely dropped his gaze to Dorothy's feet. "Hey, those are Sally's old skates!"

"Yup. And now they're Dorothy's," Grandma said proudly.

"Here," Max said, swiftly unknotting the laces and turning them into bows.

Even the top of his head is cute, Dorothy thought, admiring Max's short-cropped curls.

"You're a regular Prince Charming, Max," Grandma teased.

Dorothy felt her face grow even hotter. "Uh, thanks again," she said.

Max winked. His eyes were like those chocolate pools in the Willy Wonka movie. "No worries. I work here, so it's kind of my job to help."

Just then, Gigi, Sam, and Jade rolled up. "Ready to go?" Gigi asked, pulling Dorothy up onto her wheeled feet.

"Uh-huh, sure," Dorothy said, gripping Gigi's arm tightly. The skates fit perfectly, but she might as well have been wearing live eels on her feet for how unsteady she felt.

Grandma went to order some pizza, and the four girls rolled arm in arm to the vacant skate floor. Dorothy felt like one of those moving dollies, standing stiff and letting herself be wheeled along, but she didn't dare move her feet. Not yet. They entered the rink through a gap in the carpeted wall, and Dorothy realized that, ready or not, she was officially roller-skating. High above

51

the floor, a gigantic mirrored disco ball spun in a shaky circle, reflecting colored pools of light on the worn wood. Mellow saxophone music pumped in from two huge, precariously hung speakers.

Dorothy's ankles buckled inward and she struggled to stay linked to Sam and her two friends. *Maybe this wasn't such a good idea*, Dorothy thought, glancing over the wall to make sure Max wasn't watching her. Nope, gone. Galactic Skate was a ghost town.

The jazz song ended and the music switched to a funky bass guitar line.

"They're playin' my song!" Gigi squealed, breaking away from the chain of girls. She twirled around so she was skating backward and belted out song lyrics like a karaoke diva. "She's a super freak! Super freak! She's super freaky." She kicked one foot and then the other, bouncing and shimmying while waving her arms in the air.

"Gigi's a jam dancer," Jade yelled over the music. Gigi windmilled into a one-armed handstand and scissored her legs. "But I didn't know she was *good*."

"Good?" Gigi yelled back. She dropped back onto two

skates and weaved her feet in figure eights. "I'm the local Jam Groove Champion for my age-group."

Sam broke away and joined Gigi. "Look at me," she said, mimicking Gigi's hip-jutting, finger-pointing dance moves.

"Wow. Your sister's a natural," Jade said. "Are you sure you two have never gone skating before?"

Just then Dorothy's wheels whipped out from under her. THUD! She was suddenly staring up at the mirrored disco ball from the floor. "First time," she croaked.

Jade peeled Dorothy off the floor. When they reached the wall, Dorothy clung to it like it was the only life preserver on a sinking ship.

"Uh-oh," Jade said, staring at the front entrance. "You'll never guess who just came in."

Dorothy's head shot up and her hand went to chest. "Mom?"

"Uh, no. Were you expecting her?"

Dorothy blushed at her stupid mistake and willed her heart rate to return to normal. False alarm. No Mom. Just three girls in sparkly pink tank tops, leg warmers, and frilly sheer skirts, who began lacing up white, boot-style roller skates. Two of the skaters looked like they were probably in high school; the taller one had straight blond hair and pinched, angular features; the shorter one had curly brown ringlets and an upturned button nose. The third girl appeared to be about Dorothy's age. She tossed her blond head, sweeping a long, silky ponytail over her shoulder, then locked eyes with Dorothy.

Dorothy gasped. "Alex."

Chapter 6

"Well lookie what the cat dragged in," Gigi said, rolling over to Jade and Dorothy. Her song had ended and the quiet saxophone music had returned.

"Have you ever seen Alex here before?" Jade asked.

"Nope. But I'm never at Galactic Skate on Wednesday," Gigi replied, propping her elbows on the carpeted wall. "I only skate weekends."

Why is Alex wearing sequins? Dorothy wondered, remembering how horrified she had been when she saw Dorothy's sparkly gym outfit.

As if reading her thoughts, Alex pointed at Dorothy and then ran her finger across her throat like an invisible knife. With a flip of her ponytail, Alex rolled back out the front entrance and was gone.

Gigi frowned. "Was it just me, or did Alex just order her friends to kill us?"

Jade sighed. "We should probably just go."

"Go? No way," Gigi said, furious. "This rink doesn't belong to Alex. Besides, those prissy girls are no match for these." Gigi flattened her hands into blades and cut at the air.

"Where's Sam?" Dorothy said, suddenly feeling protective. She located her on the other side of the rink doing cartwheels. Sam wobbled on her wheels when she landed, but for a novice skater, the trick was impressive.

The tall, pinched-face girl swooped into the rink right next to Sam. "Nice cartwheel, midget," she called out, her voice echoing across the skate floor. She circled Sam like a shark.

The short, curly-haired girl skated in after. "Of course it would look better if it was more like this," she said, doing a perfect cartwheel followed up by a tight spin.

"Or this," the taller girl said, doing three consecutive

cartwheels, then twirling around Sam like a wicked ballerina on wheels.

"Leave her alone!" Dorothy shouted.

"We're just giving her a free lesson," the tall girl sneered. She grabbed Sam's hand and dragged her away like a puppy on a leash.

"I'll give you a free lesson," Gigi said, bursting into a sprint.

Jade followed, propelling herself with long, sweeping strides.

Dorothy wobbled behind, but fell to the floor before she could get very far.

"Where do you think you're going?" the shorter skater asked, suddenly appearing behind Dorothy and grabbing her collar.

"Let me go!" Dorothy shrieked.

The girl laughed and dragged Dorothy backward across the worn wood floor. "Help me!" Sam yelled.

Dorothy tore at the skater's hand, but the grip on her shirt was too tight. Dorothy grabbed for anything she could reach and yanked. The girl's skirt shot downward, dragging tights and leg warmers with it. The girl yelped, but held tight to Dorothy's collar. Dorothy yanked again and the skirt twirled into the skater's spinning wheels. She lost her balance and let go of Dorothy's shirt, crashing forward.

Too jittery to stand, Dorothy scrambled away on her knees.

On the other side of the rink, Gigi caught up with Sam and the tall skater. The tall girl seemed to be slowing on purpose and smiled dangerously as Gigi skated alongside her. Dorothy opened her mouth to scream, "It's a trap!" but it was already too late. Gigi thrust her hip to the right and the skater whirled out of reach. Gigi smashed into the wall like a bug hitting a windshield.

The tall girl cackled as she skated past Dorothy, dragging Sam just out of reach.

Jade shot forward, gaining on Sam and her captor. The tall skater glanced over her shoulder, taking in Jade's movements. Jade stretched out her hand and touched Sam's fingers, but the bully whipped Sam out of reach. Jade almost toppled forward, but deepened her knee bend and regained her balance. She caught up to Sam again,

but just as before, Sam was yanked out
of reach. Jade made a third attempt.
This time the skater slowed slightly
and Sam and Jade linked hands.

"Let go," Dorothy squeaked as the
threesome flew by. But
the tall girl was already
racing Sam and Jade into
an S curve that ended
in a powerful snap. Jade

lost her hold and whirled away like a tiny bird caught in
a tornado.

"Please help!" Sam cried as she was dragged past
Dorothy again.

But Dorothy was powerless, not even able to stand on
her own two skates.

With a jolt, Dorothy felt her skates being yanked
backward, and she found herself flat on her belly.

"You can't embarrass me like that and get away with
it," the short skater sneered. Her wheels were free.
Dorothy was dragged like a rag doll.

Dorothy tried to dig her nails into the wood, but she was trapped. Her eyes blurred with tears and her body went completely limp.

All of a sudden, Dorothy's legs were released as a streak of sparkly pink leotard and curly brown hair rocketed over her head. With a terrified scream, the girl smashed into the wall and nearly tumbled over the top.

Pink and black leopard-print roller skates zoomed by Dorothy's head. Dorothy blinked the tears out of her eyes and raised her head to see who had saved her. This skater was wearing a glossy black jumpsuit, just like Grandma's. And she had pink, spiky hair, just like Grandma's.

"Nobody messes with my girls!" the woman roared, pumping a fist into the air.

Dorothy shook her head. *It can't be!* But it was—Grandma Sally racing toward Sam and the tall skater, her body curved forward, arms bent at her elbows, even faster on roller skates than she was behind the wheel of Dead Betty.

"What the?" Jade said, still looking dizzy and disoriented.

"Go, Granny, go!" Gigi cheered.

"Back off, old lady," the bully yelled, releasing Sam.

"You stay put, cupcake," Grandma said, tousling Sam's hair as she flew by.

The tall girl raced around the rink, looking nervously over her shoulder as Grandma gained on her. In no time, Grandma caught up with the skater and wrapped both arms around her waist in a bear hug. The girl twisted out of the hold and shoved Grandma away.

"You'll regret this, old woman," she barked.

"And you'll regret callin' me an old woman," Grandma yelled, catching the girl's wrists in her hands. Grandma whipped the girl into a spin, twirling around faster and faster until the girl's feet nearly left the floor. Grandma let go and the skater spun through the air like a detached helicopter propeller, landing hard on the wood floor with a loud "woomph!"

Just then, the fat, balding man who had sold them

their entrance passes stormed onto the rink floor. "What's going on here?" he boomed.

"It's okay, Uncle Enzo," Max said, rolling up beside him. "I'll handle this."

"You better," the heavy man grumbled, marching away in a huff.

Sam was still shaking, tears rolling down her face as Jade and Gigi delivered her into Dorothy's arms. Dorothy held her little sister tightly. "I'm sorry, Sam," she whispered. "I'm so, so sorry."

Grandma skated over to the group of girls. "We creamed them!" she said, holding out her hand for a high five.

"Actually, only *you* creamed them," Gigi said, giving Grandma's hand a halfhearted smack. "*We* were getting slaughtered before you showed up."

"Sorry 'bout that, girls. Max was helping me with my hot new skates. I didn't know you all were in trouble."

"But...how did you do that?" Sam asked.

"Didn't you know?" Max said, joining them. His eyes twinkled in the disco ball's reflected light. "Your grandma is roller derby legend Shotgun Sally. She led her team to more championship wins than any other derby team in history."

"And don't forget my record for most times in the penalty box," Grandma bragged.

"Roller derby?" Dorothy said, still stunned. "Why have I never heard this before?"

"Could you teach us?" Jade pleaded.

"Seriously, G-ma," Gigi said. "Your moves are *wicked*."

"Not tonight, guys," Max said. "I'm afraid I have to kick you out for fighting. Uncle's rules. You can come back tomorrow and practice if you like." Max gave Dorothy a crooked smile and Dorothy blushed.

"You're letting them come back?" the taller skater said, limping out of the rink. "You'll never see *me* in this dump again."

"Me, either," the shorter bully whimpered, pulling herself up the wall.

Max shrugged. "Fine by me."

As Dorothy's group exited the rink and headed for the car, Sam pointed up to the fist-pumping red-haired woman in the mural. "That's you, isn't it Grandma?"

Grandma winked. "Well, you didn't hear that from me. But if you girls are interested in learning roller derby, I might know a little old lady who can teach you the ropes."

Gigi was walking ahead toward the car and stopped so quickly Jade ran into her back. "Hey!" Jade said.

"Did you just say you would teach us to play roller derby? Be our coach? Help us start a team?" Gigi asked, shocked.

"Uh, well, I didn't exactly say all that, but, yes, I do believe I would," said Grandma. "Dorth? What do you think?"

Dorothy's cell phone was burning a hole in her chest. Her mom would disown her if she knew, but right then it felt like she'd practically already done that. "Yes!" Dorothy yelled.

Chapter 7

The next morning, Dorothy strapped on her roller skates and waved good-bye to Sam and Grandma. She was not riding to school in that hearse ever again.

"Did Mom call yet?" Sam called from the doorstep.

"Uh, not yet!" Dorothy called back. And thank goodness. Dorothy wasn't looking forward to that conversation. Not now that she had roller skates.

"Okay," Sam said, sounding hurt. "Have a good day."

"You, too!" Dorothy called, trying her best to sound cheerful. Sam must really be missing Mom. "I'm sure she'll call soon!" Dorothy added, trying to sound hopeful.

Dorothy pushed the sadness from her mind and took

in a deep breath. It was a beautiful, crisp autumn morning and Dorothy was feeling brave. She had a cute new outfit, new friends, and awesome skates, and Grandma had agreed to be their roller derby coach—on the condition that they recruit some more girls for the team. Now if she could just get the hang of this roller-skating thing, everything would be perfect.

But when Dorothy finally rolled onto the school grounds, exhausted and covered in bloody scratches from a nasty tangle with a rosebush, she wasn't feeling quite as perky. And her mood went from bad to desperate as she read the hand-lettered banner that hung above the school entrance.

"Frappit, frappit, frappit," Dorothy repeated to herself as she dashed behind the hedge that surrounded the school grounds. So much had happened since yesterday morning that the whole dodgeball incident had completely slipped her mind. And now it seemed that she was at the center of one of the Pompoms' stupid awareness projects.

Dorothy's skates snagged over roots and rocks as

she tramped behind the hedge. She worked her way around to the back of the building, looking for a rear entrance. As she rounded the corner of the soccer field, she heard a choir singing a heartbreaking a cappella version of "If I Die Young." She peeked over her hedge. A large group of students stood in front of the performing choir, swaying to the melancholy music, and a group of giggling Pompoms stood behind them. With horror, Dorothy realized that all the Pompoms were wearing outfits that looked suspiciously similar to her old school uniform.

Someone tapped Dorothy on the shoulder.

"Yikes!" Dorothy screamed.

"Just me," Jade whispered.

"And me," Gigi added. "Nice memorial service they're having for you."

"Nice? It's the worst thing ever," Dorothy squeaked. "I'll never live this down."

"You don't have to," Jade said with a smirk. "You're dead, remember?"

"I think I'm going to pass out," Dorothy moaned.

"Sit down, dead girl," Gigi said, brushing away some leaves to make a smooth spot on the ground. "Take some deep breaths."

Jade made a peephole in the hedge's branches. "Shhh. They're starting the service."

The Pompoms were out front now, and one of them stepped up and cleared her throat. "Dearly beloved, we are gathered here to remember our close and personal friend, Darby." There was a pause as one of the other Pompoms whispered into the speaker's ear. The speaker coughed. "I mean Dorothy. She was an inspiration to all

of us. She didn't care how lame her clothes were, she wore them anyway. She didn't care how frizzy her hair was; she refused to condition it anyway. And when she threw a dodgeball at the most popular girl in school— sweet, beautiful Alexandra (who is too devastated to be with us this morning), well, that was just plain stupid, but you have to admit, kind of brave, too. We will all miss you, Dorky." Another pause and cough. "Dorothy. So next time, think twice about playing dodgeball, people, because you, too, could kill yourself, especially if you're a clumsy dork like...What's-Her-Face. The end."

"Who you callin' dork?" Gigi yelled, standing up behind the hedge.

"Dorothy's not a dork," Jade added, popping up next to Gigi.

"And I'm not clumsy!" Or at least that's what Dorothy had planned to say. But instead she tripped over a stick, crashed through the bushes, and screamed like a banshee as she charged toward the gaping group of mourners.

"She's alive!" the speaker bellowed into the microphone.

"Back from the dead!" another Pompom screamed.

"ZOMBIE! She's going to eat our brains!" another girl shrieked.

The audience scattered and the Pompoms ran away screaming. Dorothy rocketed out of control for several more feet, until one of her wheels caught on a sprinkler head. She flipped once and landed flat on her back, skates in the air.

"Good luck finding any brains with that bunch," Jade said flatly, offering Dorothy a hand. "You'll starve."

Gigi broke out into loud, snort-filled laughter. "Nice entrance, Dorothy. Or should I call you the Undead Redhead?"

After the craziness from the memorial service had worn off, Dorothy's day actually went pretty smoothly. Ms. Nailer made the whole class run laps as punishment for "disgracing the name of dodgeball," but since the Pompoms ignored Dorothy the whole class period, Dorothy didn't mind too much.

Besides, she thought, *running is good training for roller derby, right?*

Between classes, Dorothy received smiles and high fives, and heard things like, "nice prank, Undead Redhead," and "Way to embarrass the Pompoms!"

When the final bell rang, Dorothy went to retrieve her roller skates from her locker.

"Hi, Twinkle Toes," she said cheerily to the centipede sticker as she entered her locker combo. The door opened easily. "Hugs 'n' Kisses to you, too!" she said to the big lips that greeted her on the inside of the locker.

"No. No! NO!" someone started to yell. "That locker is OFF limits!"

"What?" Dorothy said, turning around to see Alex glaring at her.

"What part of 'off limits' don't you understand?" Alex said, slamming Dorothy's locker shut with a loud *WANG*. "It's supposed to be…broken. You can't just… open it and use it. It's…it's…"

"Not yours," Gigi said, placing a firm hand on Alex's shoulder.

Alex knocked Gigi's hand away. "Locker number thirteen is NOT available for ANYONE. And especially not for her!" she said, pointing at Dorothy.

"But Mr. Pretty Penguin and I are getting along so well," Dorothy said.

Alex's face twisted into something so furious and miserable, Dorothy almost felt sorry for her.

71

With an exasperated huff, Alex turned her back on Gigi and Dorothy and stormed away. Over her shoulder she yelled, "I'll get you, Dorothy."

Dorothy didn't miss a beat. "And my little dog, too?"

"Nice one," Gigi said, giving Dorothy a high five.

"Thanks," Dorothy said. "But I thought the Wicked Witch of the Pompoms was supposed to be absent today."

"And you were supposed to be dead, remember?" Gigi wrapped an arm around Dorothy's shoulder. "You're just a big ol' trouble magnet, you know that?"

Dorothy giggled. "I know. Speaking of trouble, are you ready for our first derby practice tonight?"

"Girl!" Gigi said, bumping Dorothy with her hip. "I was born ready. And just wait until you see who I recruited for our team."

Chapter 8

"Giddy-up!" Grandma howled as she raced Dead Betty through Galactic Skate's nearly vacant parking lot. The car bounded in and out of the minefield of potholes. "Just like ridin' a buckin' bronco!" Grandma crooned in a cowboy drawl.

"Yee-haw!" Sam said, unlatching her seat belt to enjoy the full effect of bouncing around inside the hearse.

I can't believe Sam is starting to enjoy Grandma's driving! Dorothy thought, giving her sister a dirty look. Dorothy's seat belt bit at her waist, and her insides jumped up and down like a sewing machine needle. "J-j-j-ust park all r-r-ready!"

"Whoa, girl," Grandma said, slamming on the brakes. Sam tumbled forward and giggled as they came to a stop directly in front of the main entrance. They were parked in a loading-only space.

Grandma grabbed a hot pink cowboy hat off the passenger seat and climbed out of the car.

"Do you have to wear that thing inside?" Dorothy asked.

Grandma waved the cowboy hat at Dorothy. "This little ol' thing? I wouldn't look much like a cowgirl without it, now would I?" she said, popping the hat onto her head.

Dorothy shrugged. Grandma was wearing black-and-white cow-print chaps, hot pink cowboy boots, and a bolo tie with a black widow spider frozen inside clear resin. The hat really wasn't worth fighting over.

"I think Grandma looks...rootin' tootin'!" Sam said enthusiastically as she followed Dorothy out the car door.

"Don't encourage her," Dorothy grumbled.

A green Subaru station wagon rolled up next to the hearse. The front passenger door opened, and Gigi climbed out carrying a pair of roller skates. "Thanks, Mom," she said, bumping the door closed.

The back door opened and Jade appeared, hooked her messenger bag over her shoulder, and strolled toward Dorothy. Dorothy was already headed to the entrance when she heard happy squeals. Dorothy spun around and saw Dinah exit the Subaru and bound after them. "This place is supercool," Dinah said, hopping up and down. "I want a derby outfit just like that," she added, pointing at the painting of Grandma in her tiny shorts. "I've never roller-skated, but I'm probably going to be awesome."

"Settle down there, darlin'," Grandma said, looking nervously up at the wall as she pulled two large leopard-print duffel bags out of the back of the hearse.

Dorothy leaned into Gigi. "*This* is your derby recruit?" she whispered. Dorothy was starting to wonder if Dinah was a few nuggets short of a Happy Meal.

"Sure. She's really excited, see?" Gigi whispered back. Dinah was shuffling around the sidewalk, pretending she was roller-skating.

Dinah sang, "I'm a roller derby girl! Derby, derby, roller, yeah!"

Dorothy shrugged. She had to admit that Dinah's enthusiasm was pretty contagious. Soon everyone except Grandma joined Dinah in a round of "I'm a roller derby girl! Derby, derby, roller, yeah!"

Suddenly from high above, a chunk of wall broke away from the mural, smashing into a million pieces just inches away from where the singing girls stood. Everyone scattered, screaming, while Grandma glared angrily up at the painting. Where there had once been a beautiful mouth on the Asian woman's face, a gaping hole remained, frozen in a silent scream.

"Shame on you, Eva," Grandma growled, her cowboy accent gone.

"Eva?" Dorothy bleated. "Who's Eva?"

"Eva Disaster, dear. She's probably just sensitive about us doing roller derby here."

Max appeared from behind the double doors. "Come on, Sally. Don't scare those girls with ghost stories."

"Eva's...a ghost?" Dorothy asked, staring up at the hole in the wall as the other girls rushed into Galactic Skate through the open doors.

"Died in my arms, hon," Grandma said, shaking her head as she steered Dorothy into the building.

"How sad," Jade said as the group headed toward the skate rentals. The wrinkled old man was snoozing behind the rocket-shaped desk. He didn't look like he had moved since yesterday.

"Still," Gigi said, "Eva shouldn't be throwing bricks at us. That Enzo guy should hire an exorcist or something."

"Or a brick mason," Max grumbled. "This old building is falling apart. Ghosts are the least of our problems."

"I saw a ghost once," Dinah chirped. "He was all like 'Help me, Dinah!,' and I was all like 'Ahh! Scary ghost!'—but it just turned out to be my dad covered in pancake batter."

Everyone just stared at Dinah.

"So," Max said, changing the subject. "I've got good news. I talked to my uncle and he said you could practice here for free in exchange for doing a few odd jobs around the place. And he said you could use the old equipment in the basement."

"That's my boyfriend!" Grandma said, giving Max a

fist bump. "So how 'bout you and Dorothy go down and get those boxes?"

"Grandma," Dorothy hissed, embarrassed.

Max draped a friendly arm over Dorothy's shoulder. "Don't worry," he whispered. "I'll protect you from that scary ghost."

The door to the basement was located behind the shelves of skates. It was slightly ajar, and Dorothy could smell decaying wood and musty earth. The door creaked when Max pushed it open, revealing a staircase that descended into darkness. Max flipped on a tiny flashlight and trotted down the stairs ahead of Dorothy. Dorothy tried to ignore the chilly sensation that washed over her skin and made the hair rise on her arms. She focused on the flashlight's bouncing beam and stayed close behind Max.

Something scuttled over Dorothy's feet. Dorothy screeched and tripped forward, crashing into Max's back. Max caught his balance, but just barely. His flashlight popped out of his hand and skipped down the staircase, the beam spinning erratically until it hit the bottom and went black.

"You okay, Dorth?" Max whispered in the darkness.

"Something's down here!" Dorothy whimpered, arms wrapped tight around Max's broad shoulders.

Max chuckled. "Probably just a ghost."

"You're making fun of me!" Dorothy said, releasing Max with a little shove.

"Hey! It was just a joke," Max said, steadying himself. "I should have warned you about the mice."

"Mice?!" Dorothy squeaked, hugging him again.

"Let's just find our way to the bottom," Max said, helping Dorothy down onto his step. "There's a light down there."

Dorothy felt a rush of fear and excitement as Max took her hand in the blackness. When they reached the concrete floor at the bottom of the stairs, Max yanked on a string and a single bare bulb came to life above his head. The basement was small, lined with shadowy shelves that held dusty cardboard boxes of various sizes. Max gave Dorothy a crooked grin. "See? No scary ghosts."

Dorothy cleared her throat. "So, um. How did Eva Disaster die?"

Max picked up a box marked HELMETS and looked inside. "I actually don't know. Your grandma won't talk about it much. Sally and Eva were on the same derby team, but they were rivals. Eva died almost thirty years ago, during the Halloween championship bout."

"But, what kind of died?" Dorothy asked, her eyes wide. "Like accident died or…"

Max sighed and met Dorothy's gaze. "It wasn't natural causes, if that's what you mean."

"Murdered?" Chills crept up and down Dorothy's spine. "But by who?"

"Hey!" Grandma's voice echoed down the staircase, making Dorothy jump. "If you two are done smoochin', we need that equipment up here!"

"Right," Max said, handing the helmet box to Dorothy. Max picked up two other boxes and followed Dorothy as she carefully made her way up the stairs.

Eva murdered! Right here at Galactic Skate. No wonder the place is haunted!

Chapter 9

The equipment wasn't heavy, but the box was an awkward shape. Dorothy managed to carry it up the stairs safely...until the last step. She lost her footing and fumbled the box, sending dusty helmets spilling through the open doorway. Dorothy fell onto the box and a terrible, high-pitched squeal from inside the crushed cardboard made her dash to the safety of the rental desk.

"Mouse!" Dorothy yelped, shaking her legs and patting at her body wildly, trying to get rid of the sensation of a thousand tiny rodent feet clawing at her skin.

"Mouse dance!" Dinah shouted. She duplicated

Dorothy's kicking feet and crazy arms, and finished with a twirl and jazz hands.

The wrinkled old man at the rental desk opened one milky eye and went back to snoring a moment later.

Grandma laughed. "Save some of that energy for practice, girls."

Max set his boxes next to the rental desk and picked up Dorothy's helmets before going to set up the rink.

"We've got a big surprise exercise planned, so no peeking," Grandma told the girls. "Just suit up and meet us at the rink in fifteen minutes."

Dorothy, Gigi, Jade, Dinah, and Sam peered down at the crumpled helmet box.

Sam wrinkled her nose. "Do you really think there's a mouse in there?"

"Naw," Gigi said, digging into the box. "Dorothy's just jumpy because of that ghost."

Dorothy rubbed the back of her neck. Maybe Gigi was right. She was feeling a little freaked out about Eva.

Jade picked up a dusty helmet by the strap and held it out like a dead turtle. "This stuff needs a major makeover."

82

Dorothy took the helmet from her. "It might be okay," she said, using her finger to draw a black heart in the dust. She placed the helmet onto her head and tiny black pebbles fell out.

"Uh, mouse poop, Dorothy," Gigi said.

Dorothy instantly flung the helmet off her head and slapped her hair like it was on fire. "Ew! Eww! Ewww!"

"I got this one," Jade said, pulling a can of disinfectant spray out of her messenger bag. Wielding it like a gun, she zapped the offending helmet and then kicked the helmet box onto its side, FBI style. Six tiny gray mice skipped out of the box. Jade shot at them with disinfectant while Dorothy, Sam, and Dinah screamed.

When the mice were gone, the girls gingerly sorted through the boxes and washed off the equipment in the ladies' room. Once they were dressed in pads and helmets, they rolled to the rink.

Dorothy felt extra lucky to have Grandma's old skates now. They were a hundred times nicer than anything in the boxes. Sam had to wear rental skates because her feet were so small. She said she didn't mind—Grandma said she couldn't be on the team until she was older, anyway—but Dorothy knew that Sam was secretly jealous.

When the group rolled up to the skate floor, Dorothy's jaw dropped. The rink had been trashed. It was covered in old, broken objects: chewed-up squeaky toys, a wooden leg in an umbrella stand, cracked bowling pins, a broken coffeemaker, and a wilting flower arrangement with a banner that read REST IN PIECES, among other things.

"Uh, somebody call *Hoarders*," Gigi said.

Dinah clapped her hands and squealed. "It's a yard sale! I LOVE yard sales. I call dibs on the false teeth!"

Dorothy made a face. Those teeth were just the kind of thing Grandma liked to collect from the mortuary.

"I don't think it's a yard sale, Dinah."

"Dorothy's right," Grandma said, swerving and hopping

over objects to reach the girls. She was still wearing her cowboy hat, but she had replaced her hot pink boots with leopard-print skates. "This here is Grandma Sally's deluxe obstacle course. If you can survive skating through this mess," she said, sweeping her arm across the rink like a cheesy game show host, "you'll be ready to avoid obstacles that block your path during a bout."

Dinah raised her hand. "What's a bout?"

"A game, hon," Grandma said. "It's what we call our matches."

Dorothy raised her hand, too, wanting to know how skating through garbage could possibly help her. She couldn't even skate in a straight line yet.

"Enough questions," Grandma said. "Let's do this!" She ordered the girls to start at either side of the rink. Gigi and Jade went left while Dinah and Dorothy headed to the right.

Dorothy felt like a plump pig at a barbecue picnic as she used the wall to guide her to the starting spot. Did Grandma really expect her to skate through this mess safely? The objects glinted like jagged teeth in the disco ball's reflected light.

Max's lopsided smile appeared over the wall behind Dorothy. "Deep breath, Dorth. Just take it slow and you'll do fine."

Deep breath? Dorothy thought. *I'm going to need a lot more than breath for this exercise.*

Grandma handed Sam her silver whistle. "All righty, girls! Let's see how you do."

On Grandma's cue, Sam gave the whistle a shrill blast.

"Watch and learn, people," Gigi said, dashing into the rink. Gigi made figure eights around a rusty can opener, a broken wire whisk, and a man's leather shoe. She weaved around a pyramid of soda cans, jumped over a birdcage, and cartwheeled through the scattering of warped textbooks.

She was bouncing through a line of bicycle inner tubes when Grandma yelled, "Peripherals, Gigi. Watch that backside!" and lobbed her duffel bag.

Dorothy gasped as the bag hit Gigi in the shoulder and knocked her off balance. Gigi tripped, tumbled forward, and became tangled in the old jump rope. With a "yowch!" and an "eek eek eek!" Gigi wheeled over a prickly hairbrush and a scattering of jacks. She continued to roll as items stuck to her hair, her clothing, and the frayed rope until she finally crashed into an electric guitar with an earsplitting *bah-WANG!*

Gigi spat a silk flower out of her mouth. "I'm going to wring your wrinkly neck, G-ma!" She struggled to stand, but the rope was hopelessly tangled around her arms and ankles.

"Sorry about that, hon," Grandma said, trying to suppress a chuckle. "Guess I didn't know my own strength. I'll send in some help."

Grandma nodded to Sam, who blew the whistle.

"My turn," Jade said, sweeping into the rink. But instead of going to Gigi's rescue, she raced along the wall's edge where the path looked clear, her eyes focused on the finish line.

She didn't get far.

"Marbles?" Jade yelped, tripping and skipping through tiny balls. When she was just inches away from clear floor, one of the balls caught under her wheels and she careened out of control.

Gigi was right in Jade's way, round bottom in the air, still impossibly tangled in the jump rope.

"Move your big booty!" Jade screamed.

"Who you callin' big, you—" Gigi didn't have a chance to finish her insult. Jade smashed into Gigi's backside, and they rolled into a spaghetti-like heap.

Grandma shook her head, disappointed. "So much for teamwork," she muttered.

Gigi and Jade were too busy fighting and name-calling to work their way out of the mess.

Jade should have helped Gigi, right? Dorothy thought.

Grandma elbowed Sam, and the whistle trilled again.

Dorothy looked nervously from Grandma to Dinah. If talented skaters like Gigi and Jade couldn't make it through the course, why should she even try?

Dinah smiled and patted Dorothy on the shoulder. "It's okay. I'll go first," she said. "It'll be fun. You'll see!" With a cheery wave, Dinah clopped out into the obstacle course like a horse on roller skates.

Dorothy breathed a sigh of relief. "Thanks, Dinah."
She was glad the goofy girl had joined the team after all.
Dinah was strange, but nice, too.

"What's that girl up to now?" Max asked, resting his
dimpled chin on his hands.

Dinah was headed right for the umbrella stand…and
the wooden leg.

Dorothy tilted her head to look at Max. "Knowing
Dinah, she's going to get that wooden leg and ride it like
a horse."

Max laughed. "Sounds about right."

Dinah clippety-clopped over a snow shovel and
around a one-eyed teddy bear. Arriving in front of the
umbrella stand, she picked up the wooden leg, swung
her leg over it, and continued roller-clopping through
the debris.

Max chuckled. "Nice call, Dorth. Do you always know
what people are going to do?"

Dorothy shrugged. "I guess so. Sometimes, anyway."

There were three short whistle blasts and Dorothy
looked over at Grandma.

"I've seen enough!" Grandma barked. "Get your sorry behinds over here. We need to talk."

"Guess I better untie Jade and Gigi," Max said, swinging his legs up and over the wall.

Once Gigi and Jade were free, the small team gathered around Grandma.

"You call yourselves a roller derby team?" Grandma said. The fluorescent light directly above the group flickered like a storm cloud. "That was the most pathetic exercise I've seen in all my days of skating."

"Grandma?" Dorothy said. "Don't you think an obstacle course is a little advanced for our first practice?"

"Nonsense," Grandma said. "This course is easier than picking a good skate name, if you ask me."

"Skate name?" Jade said, not looking up from the red rope burns on her arms.

Grandma slapped her forehead. "You girls really don't know anything about derby, do you?"

"Duh," Gigi said. "First practice. Never done this before, remember?"

"A skate name is like a nickname," Max said. "It's what they call you on the track."

"Right," Grandma said. "And you want something smart, sassy. A name that says you're a force to be reckoned with. Take my old derby name, for instance. Shotgun Sally." Grandma whipped her hands out of her pockets like a quick-draw gunslinger and squeezed off a couple pretend rounds. "And I didn't just get that name because I carried a loaded revolver in my bra, you know."

Dorothy shuddered at the thought of Grandma with a loaded gun.

"Don't worry," Gigi said, giving Dorothy an encouraging pat on the back. "You already have a great name, remember?"

"Like what?" said a familiar mocking voice. "The Undead Redhead?" Everyone turned to see Alex skating into the rink. She was wearing her white roller skates, but instead of a sparkly leotard and tutu, she was wearing pink sweatpants and a simple V-cut T-shirt. She weaved casually through the strewn objects.

"You have some nerve showing your face here," Jade said, her mouth pulled into a thin, rigid line.

Alex swerved away from Dorothy's group. "My da—my parents say I have to practice here. So we're going to have to share the rink."

"Share?" Dorothy said. She could hear the blood pounding in her ears. "After what your friends did to us yesterday?"

"I have no idea what you're talking about," Alex said flatly. She turned her back on the group, flipping her silky blond ponytail. "I hope you're going to clean this mess up now. I've got nationals to train for."

"I think it's time to teach Little Miss Perfect a lesson," Gigi growled, launching herself after Alex.

"Hold up," Max said, a hand on Gigi's shoulder. "Alex does have the right to be here. And if you get into another fight, Uncle Enzo will kick all of you out of Galactic Skate for good."

Grandma blew her whistle, making the girls jump. "Okay, team, that's practice. Go pick up the rink while I get the pizza."

Dinah and Sam followed orders and started gathering up items.

"Yo, Shotgun," Gigi said, her hands on her hips. "What do you mean practice is over?"

"Yeah," Jade said, yanking off her helmet. "You still haven't told us anything about the game. Like how it's played, the rules…"

Grandma laughed and elbowed Max in the ribs. "Rules? You hear that? They're worried about the rules."

"Seriously, G-ma," Gigi said. "Don't you think we should know something about the sport? We're going to compete, right?"

"Don't you worry," Grandma said. "Max here is an expert. We'll get you all up to speed soon enough."

"And what about me?" Dorothy added quietly. "I didn't go."

"Go where, hon? You gotta pee?" Grandma asked.

Dorothy's cheeks flushed. "No, Grandma. The exercise. Everyone went through the obstacle course except me." It wasn't like Dorothy had wanted to skate through that mess, but she didn't want to be left out, either.

"No prob, Dot," Grandma said. "You can do the

obstacle course on Monday. I'm guessing the other girls will want to try it, too."

"What other girls?" Gigi asked.

Grandma narrowed her eyes. "Don't tell me you don't have more recruits? We can't compete with just four girls."

Dorothy gave Jade and Gigi a worried look. Where were they going to find more girls crazy enough to join a roller derby team? Especially this team.

"We've got it covered," Gigi said. "I'm already an awesome recruiter."

Jade and Dorothy glanced over to where Dinah was attaching a dog collar to the wooden leg. Dinah looked up, smiled, and patted the leg on the foot.

"Can I keep him? Pleeease?"

Chapter 10

The next morning, Dorothy got up early to train before school. It was finally Friday, but Dorothy was too worried about Monday's practice to be excited for the weekend.

She pulled on some clothes, grabbed her skates, and headed downstairs to the old embalming room.

The large cement room was the perfect place to skate—if you ignored the spiders and didn't think too much about the odd tools hanging from the wall or the drain at the center of the floor.

Dorothy's skin crawled as she pushed a metal embalming table up against the wall next to a slow-dripping sink. How many dead bodies had been down here? Hundreds? More?

Pull it together, she told herself. *Focus on skating.*

Dorothy laced her skates and took a lap around the cement room. Her arms flailed wildly as she tried to keep both skates on the ground. Wobble, wobble, CRASH!

After several wipeouts, she found a small wheeled cart and used it like an old lady's walker to push herself around the room. The cart's small size forced her to bend her knees, and she found that she was instantly more balanced.

After one lap with the cart, she tried skating without it. To her surprise, she found that it wasn't the cart that was giving her balance, it was the bend in her knees! Soon Dorothy was able to swing her arms in time with her strides, too, and she had picked up some speed.

After an hour of practice, it was time to head to school. Dorothy grabbed a cold Toaster Tart and waved good-bye to Sam, Grandma, and Morti, who were practicing Tai Chi in the parlor.

The morning air was chilly but invigorating. Autumn leaves made a satisfying crunching sound under Dorothy's skates. She practiced hopping over sidewalk cracks and weaving through rocks and gravel, and before she knew it, she was skating into the J. Elway parking lot. No falls, no scraped knees, and no tangles with rosebushes.

And I still have time to catch up on homework, she thought as she rolled inside the school.

The halls were nearly empty. She passed a janitor pushing a broom and a couple of teachers getting ready for class. She didn't see any students. At least not until she turned the corner to her bank of lockers. Someone was standing in front of locker number 13. Someone with silky blond hair. And she was scratching the door with a house key.

Dorothy gasped. "Alex?"

Alex whipped around, looking like a toddler caught with her hand in the cookie jar.

"What are you doing to my stickers?" Dorothy yelled.

"They're not your...They..." Alex stammered, her

cheeks turning red. Alex's jaw snapped closed and she curled her manicured fingers into trembling fists.

Dorothy's mouth fell open. She was so surprised it took a second to register what Alex was doing.

Just as suddenly, Alex let out a tiny shriek, and with a flip of her ponytail, she ran away.

"Coward!" Dorothy yelled, slamming into her locker. Dorothy pushed off the cold metal door and skated after Alex, but an elderly teacher stuck his balding head out of his classroom door and frowned.

Dorothy hit the brakes, smiled nervously at the teacher, and skated back to her locker. She just wanted to get to the bottom of Alex's issues.

Dorothy examined the locker door. Thin scratches scarred several of the sparkly stickers. Dorothy ran her finger over the penguin's sash, where the lines were heaviest.

What does Alex have against Mr. Pretty? Dorothy thought. Fortunately, none of the scratches were very deep. The stickers had been sealed to the locker with a heavy coating of some sort of clear glue. Whoever had put them there had made sure that the Mr. Pretty wasn't going anywhere anytime soon.

Dorothy dialed in her combo and opened the door. As always, the big lips smiled back at her.

Dorothy stuck her tongue out at the sticker. "More like Slugs 'n' Hisses," she grumbled.

In P.E., Dorothy was determined to confront Alex, but she didn't get the chance. Ms. Nailer ordered the class to jump rope for the whole period. After only a few minutes of jumping, the Pompoms were excused to go to the library to work on their next awareness project: Drool Ain't Cool. Wear a Bib, Zombie People.

Jade and Dorothy took a break from jumping to watch the Pompoms trot merrily out of the gymnasium.

"Zombie bibs? That's the stupidest thing I've ever heard," Jade said.

One of the Pompoms stuck her tongue out at Dorothy.

Dorothy scowled back. "It's not a real project. They're making fun of me."

"Why?" Jade asked. "Because you're the Undead Redhead?"

"Yeah. Something like that," Dorothy said.

Whoosh! CRACK!

Dorothy and Jade yelped, spinning around to see Ms. Nailer brandishing a jump rope like a whip. Yellow teeth bared, she swung the rope over her head once and snapped it down just inches from Dorothy's toes. "Now JUMP!"

Dorothy and Jade jumped.

Ms. Nailer snorted and raised the whip again. "With jump ropes?"

Thirty minutes later they were still jumping rope. Dorothy's lungs burned, and her knees felt like Jell-O. If she kept this up much longer, she would collapse. She was sure of it.

Fortunately, the class got an unexpected break when the door to the girls' dressing room swung open. A girl the size of a refrigerator strutted into the gymnasium. She was wearing a black leather jacket, and her hair was slicked back like that of a 1950s greaser.

Ms. Nailer stepped in front of the big girl, blocking her way. The girl took a bold step forward and glared down into the gym teacher's sour face.

"Nice of you to show up, Dee," Ms. Nailer growled through gritted teeth.

"Nice of you to let dead animals live in your mouth," Dee said, leaning back and waving her hand in front of her nose.

Juana slunk farther back into her corner while Jade gave Dorothy a conspiratorial smile. Dinah, Ruth, and Lizzy giggled.

"Quiet!" Ms. Nailer barked, scanning the floor with her angry, beady eyes.

Everyone quickly went back to jumping rope.

Ms. Nailer turned back to Dee. "It's not going to work this time, Dee. Get a rope."

The girl shook a meaty fist in Ms. Nailer's direction.

"Oh, come on, Nailer. You know you want to send me to detention."

"Congratulations, Dee. You've just earned that detention," Ms. Nailer said.

Dee grunted and retracted her fist. A bead of nervous sweat slid down her wide nose. "Fine. I'll be on my way then."

"No chance," Ms. Nailer sneered. "You're not getting out of my class this time. You'll be going to after-school detention." Ms. Nailer pointed to the jumping students. "Now get that rope."

Dorothy exchanged looks with Jade. "Who is she?" Dorothy mouthed.

Jade crossed her wrists and jumped through the twist a few times. "Dee's the toughest girl in school. And she ditches a lot. They say she'll do just about anything if she thinks it will get her out of class."

Dorothy bit her lip and stared nervously at Dee.

Dee shot Dorothy a menacing look. "You want a knuckle sandwich, twerp?"

Chapter 11

The cafeteria was filled with noisy students, but none of them were in line for chicken-fried steak.

More for me, Dorothy thought. *I'm so hungry I could eat my skates.* Between jumping rope for an hour and skating to school, she was almost too famished to lift the tray.

"What do you think you're doing?" Gigi said, yanking the tray from Dorothy's hands. "Even I don't eat the cafeteria food."

"What else is there?" Dorothy asked.

"Salad," Gigi said. She gestured to a table at the back of the cafeteria, where Jade was already nibbling on a forkful of leafy green vegetables.

Dorothy shook her head. "No thanks. I need some-thing more than rabbit food."

Gigi shrugged and handed back Dorothy's tray. "Suit yourself."

Dorothy's appetite vanished as a wide-smiling, gap-toothed, elderly lunch lady slapped a mysterious meat patty covered in gravy onto her plate. It could have been broiled frog for all Dorothy knew. Dorothy trudged her way through the maze of lunch tables, wishing she had taken Gigi's advice. No way could she eat...whatever that was.

She was halfway across the cafeteria when she felt her feet come out from under her. Her tray crashed to the floor and Dorothy smashed face-first into a pile of instant potatoes. Green beans and bits of meat splashed everywhere.

"Frappit," Dorothy spluttered. Her face felt hot, either from potatoes or embarrassment, she wasn't sure. In her potato-blurred peripheral vision, she saw a foot slip back under the table to her right.

Dorothy wiped potatoes out of her eyes and got to her feet. "Who tripped me?" she yelled. A group of smirking

Pompoms stared back at her. Alex was among them, looking particularly guilty with her eyes glued to her crust-free sandwich.

"Did you hear something?" one of the Pompoms asked.

"Nope," said another. "Probably just a ghost."

The Pompoms giggled.

"She's not a ghost," a cheery voice said. Dorothy looked to her left and saw Dinah grinning up at her.

Dinah was sharing a table with Lizzy and Juana, neither of whom returned Dorothy's gaze. Lizzy was busy making notes in her Space Fleet manual, and Juana was quietly repacking her uneaten lunch into a paper bag.

Dinah hopped out of her seat and bounced over to Dorothy. She wiped a finger across Dorothy's cheek and took a lick. "See?" she said, smacking her lips. "Not a ghost. Just mashed potatoes."

"Nobody asked you, you little peon," a Pompom sneered.

Dinah's childlike grin melted into a pout. "Little? Peon?" she repeated. As the insult sunk in, anger sparked behind Dinah's eyes. Next thing Dorothy knew, Dinah was punching and kicking at the air. "Boom!" she shouted. "Pow! Pow! Kablooie! I may be small, but I'm fierce. You mess with me and I'll explode."

"Take cover," one of the Pompoms joked. "I think Dinah's gonna blow."

The Pompoms snickered.

"Yeah. Like dynamite," another Pompom teased. "Get it? Dinah Mite?"

"Dinah Mite?" Dinah repeated. "Dinah Mite!" She flung her arms around the Pompom who had just insulted her. "Oh my gosh. That's perfect. Did you hear that, Dorothy? I just got my roller derby name!"

DINAH-MITE!

"Um, that's great, Dinah. Let's just get out of here, okay?" Dorothy quickly scraped green beans and slippery meat off the floor and back onto her tray.

"Roller derby?" a Pompom sneered. "That's roller-skating for rednecks, right?"

"Yeah," said another. "Roller-skating is so lame."

Dorothy shot Alex a puzzled look. Alex

returned her gaze and shook her head subtly, a pleading expression flashing across her pretty face.

They don't know, Dorothy realized.

"Roller derby isn't lame," Dinah said, lifting a limp green bean from Dorothy's tray. She wagged the bean for emphasis. "It's for cool people like Dorothy, and Jade, and Gigi."

The slimy green bean squirted out of Dinah's fingers and plopped onto a Pompom's head. It clung to the girl's blond locks like a juicy caterpillar trapped in bird's nest.

"Now you're throwing food at me?" the Pompom said. She picked up a carrot stick and winged it at Dinah. Dinah ducked, and the carrot whooshed over her head, smacking Lizzy in her back.

"By Glinktar's Ax!" Lizzy exclaimed, spinning around in her seat. "Who dares violate the neutral zone?"

"Go back to your book, geek," the Pompom said.

Lizzy bared her teeth, sunlight glinting off her silver braces. "The name is Lizzy," she growled.

"Right. I remember," the Pompom said. "Lizzy the Lizard. Biggest geek ever."

107

Lizzy flew out of her seat. "That's it!" she roared. "Big lizard, you say? I'll show you a big lizard!" She stomped toward the Pompoms' table, her Godzilla-like growls echoing through the now silent cafeteria. The Pompoms squealed, and several of them dropped what they were eating.

"No, Lizzy! No!" It was Ruth, the big girl from gym class, racing across the cafeteria toward the Pompoms' table. "Calm down before you get in trouble."

"Let me do this!" Lizzy bellowed, kicking a bagel like it was a soccer ball.

The bagel landed directly under Ruth's feet and the big girl slipped on it, rocketing toward the table, arms flailing.

"Thunder Thighs!" a Pompom screamed, scrambling out of the way. "Stop now before you—"

But Ruth couldn't stop, not until she hit the edge of the table. The table legs groaned under the girl's weight. With a metallic crash, Ruth's end of the table slammed to the floor. The Pompoms fell backward from their seats as their lunches catapulted into the air. A tuna fish sandwich hit Lizzy squarely between the eyes. Lizzy tried to wipe the gooey tuna from her face, but it was no use. She couldn't see where she was going. Her foot snagged the table leg, and she fell hard and fast, right on top of Ruth.

Dorothy gasped. Both girls lay motionless in the pile of smashed food. Were they hurt? Unconscious?

After several heartbeats, Ruth opened one eye and giggled. Lizzy rolled over onto her back, peeled a pickle off her nose, and joined in her laughter with a "Snark! Snark! Snark!"

Dorothy laughed, too, relieved that the two girls were okay. The messy situation suddenly seemed hilarious.

"It's not funny!" shouted a Pompom. Her blond hair was covered in quivering globs of Jell-O. "You mutants are an embarrassment to J. Elway Middle School!"

"You're calling *us* mutants?" Ruth said before launching into a streak of hyena cackles.

Lizzy pointed at the Pompom's head. "Pretty—*snark*—funny—*snark*—coming from someone who looks like the Blob Creature from Planet Glooptar."

"What's going on here?" a deep, female voice bellowed. Ms. Nailer marched through the cafeteria entrance, her intense black eyes zeroed in on Dorothy and her sloppy lunch tray. Dorothy's laughter evaporated.

Ms. Nailer reached the table and yanked Dorothy's tray out of her hands. "Starting food fights now, are we?" Her breath stank of egg salad sandwich. "You and your band of troublemakers are in HUGE trouble."

Oh frap, Dorothy thought. What horrible thing would Ms. Nailer use for punishment now?

Dorothy clenched her jaw. "It is not our fault," she said. "The Pompoms started it. They should be in trouble, not us."

Ms. Nailer's voice dropped to a hiss. "Is that so?" Her beady eyes darted to Alex, who was covered in wriggling spaghetti noodles. "You want me to believe that the Pompoms did *this* to themselves?"

"Uh…" Dorothy was covered with food, too, but as usual, Ms. Nailer wasn't seeing her point of view.

Dorothy's eyes scanned the cafeteria for someone to back her story. She spied Juana slinking away from her table, her lunch bag clutched protectively to her chest.

Ms. Nailer followed Dorothy's gaze. "Juana! Thought you could slip away and hide, did you?"

"But she...But I—" Dorothy started. She hadn't meant to get Juana in trouble, too.

"But nothing," Ms. Nailer said. "DETENTION!"

Chapter 12

At the end of the day, Dorothy reported to Mr. Macarini's classroom. Sunshine filtered into the spacious art room through a wall of windows, but Dorothy's mood was dark. She was serving time for a food fight she hadn't started, and her bad luck was spreading. Dinah, Ruth, Lizzy, and Juana were already sitting at desks. Chunks of lettuce and deli meat still clung to the back of Ruth's and Lizzy's hair.

Dorothy chose a desk at the back of the room and sat down quietly, but the chair's feet squeaked loudly on the concrete floor.

Everyone turned to look at her. To Dorothy's surprise,

no one looked angry or disappointed. In fact, the girls were smiling.

"Detention is so cool," Dinah said. "Do you think we'll get to do crafts?"

"I'm sorry I got you all into this," Dorothy said.

"You shoulds not be sorry," Juana said, sweeping a strand of dark hair out of her eyes. "You had bravery, no?"

Me? Brave? Dorothy wondered. She had talked back to Ms. Nailer, but that seemed more stupid than brave now that everyone was in trouble.

Lizzy gave Dorothy a big, bracey smile. "Personally, I don't care if they lock me in the brig with Dracknesian Glibnofs, I'd do it all again in a nanosecond. Those Pompoms have tormented me for years. Did you see the looks on their faces when I growled at their table?"

Ruth giggled and gave Lizzy a high five. "And when I tipped it over?"

"Okay, girls. Party's over." It was Mr. Macarini entering the room. He was followed closely by the refrigerator from gym class.

Dorothy gulped. *Dee.*

Mr. Macarini ordered Dee into a chair and then sat down behind his desk. The art teacher was a middle-aged man with a handlebar mustache and long, curly hair. Dorothy had only known him for a couple days, but he was definitely her favorite teacher at J. Elway—funny and nice. But by the disappointed look on his face, Dorothy guessed that was all about to change.

"Miss Moore, front of the room, please."

Dorothy's head drooped and she walked obediently to Mr. Macarini's desk. She could feel everyone's eyes on her back.

Mr. Macarini spoke to Dorothy in a low voice. "Listen, Dorothy. I'm not a big fan of the Pompoms, either, but violence is never the answer. You should know that."

"But I didn't do anything," Dorothy mumbled.

Mr. Macarini sighed and rubbed the edge of his mustache with a thumb. "Actually, I believe you."

"You do?" Dorothy said, relief washing over her body.

"But," the teacher said, "you're still in trouble. Your friends ruined the Pompoms' lunches and destroyed that table. And you didn't stop them. It was a miracle no one was hurt."

Dorothy folded her arms across her chest. *This is so unfair!* "Come on, Mr. Macarini. I didn't tell them what to do. It's not like I'm their leader or anything. I'm just...nobody."

The teacher raised an eyebrow. "Is that so?" He nodded to the classroom.

Dorothy turned and was shocked by what she saw. With the exception of Dee (now scratching her initials into the table with a thumbnail), everyone was staring at her. Their eyes conveyed a mixture of concern and admiration, eerily reminding Dorothy of how the Pompoms gawked over Alex.

Dorothy snapped her mouth shut. *I don't get it. Why are they looking at me like that?*

"You may go back to your desk now," Mr. Macarini said softly.

Once Dorothy was back in her chair, Mr. Macarini addressed the class. "Listen up, people. I'm missing an electric ukulele concert to be here, so I expect you all to be quiet and study while I put my bachelor's degree to good use in grading these masterpieces." The teacher held up a painting that looked a lot like cat throw up.

Dorothy unzipped her backpack and took out her math homework, but she couldn't concentrate. She was still thinking about what Mr. Macarini had said. Did these girls really look up to her?

But I'm not a leader. I'm just Dorothy the freak. The Undead Redhead. Right?

Dorothy's thoughts were interrupted by the classroom intercom.

"Mr. Macarini! Mr. Macarini! Please meet animal control at your car immediately. We have a... a situation."

Mr. Macarini sprang to his feet and looked at the intercom, then back at his class. "I'll just be a minute," he said, pulling a jacket from under his desk before running to the door. "Stay put," he ordered. He pointed a warning finger at Dee. "Especially you."

The girls listened as Mr. Macarini's footsteps echoed down the hallway.

"I wonder what animal control is doing at his car," Ruth said.

"I bet bunny rabbits are trying to steal it," Dinah suggested.

Lizzy snarked. "Or lizards," she said.

Dorothy had to smile at the nerdy girl. She'd never seen Lizzy so bubbly.

"Speaking of lizards," Dorothy said, "nice Godzilla impression."

Lizzy grinned. "You can call me Geekzilla, if you'd like."

Dorothy nodded. "Okay, Geekzilla."

"Hey!" Dinah said, bouncing out of her chair. She did a happy jig that looked a lot like a potty dance. "I just had a great idea. You guys should totally join our roller derby team!"

"Roller derby?" Lizzy said, adjusting her glasses.

"Sure!" Dinah said. "You already have an awesome skate name and everything."

Dorothy cleared her throat, trying to get Dinah's attention. Dorothy liked Lizzy, but it would take more than a good name to be good at roller derby. Shouldn't they be trying to recruit athletic girls? Like the soccer players or girls from the Ultimate Frisbee team?

"The next training is Monday after school," Dinah continued, not noticing Dorothy's zip-your-lips signal. "We need more players, and you guys totally kicked butt at lunch today."

Kicked butt? Dorothy thought, thinking of the upturned table and Ruth and Lizzy laughing themselves silly in a pile of smashed food.

"My skating is decent," Lizzy said. "And I can offer strategy advice."

"I can roller-skate, too," Ruth said. "But do I have to use Thunder Thighs for my skate name? I know I'm kind of big, but…" She started to giggle, but there was something so sad about the laugh, it nearly broke Dorothy's heart.

Dorothy sighed. Poor Ruth. Was it her fault that she was bigger? She was strong, too, right? During the dodgeball game she had knocked over Pompoms like bowling pins.

"Um," Dorothy said, thinking out loud, "maybe you could go by Rolling Thunder instead?"

Ruth stopped giggling, and her eyes lit up like she had just received a Christmas present. "Rolling Thunder? Oh, Dorothy, it's an awesome skate name. Thank you!"

Oh, frap. Did I really just recruit Ruth?

Dee rocked back in her chair and propped her huge, muddy boots on the table. "Roller derby, huh?" she said. "So you guys get to hit people and stuff, right? 'Cause I like to hit stuff."

Dorothy cringed. *Not Dee. Anyone but Dee!* The beastly girl would probably break everyone like dry twigs before the team even had a chance to compete.

Before Dorothy could think of a way to talk Dee out of joining, there was a tap-tap-tap at the window. Gigi and Jade peered in, their noses pressed against the glass. Dorothy leapt out of her seat and rushed to her friends, unlocking the window and pushing it open.

"Jailbreak!" Gigi said. She grabbed Dorothy by the shoulders and pulled her halfway through the opening.

Dorothy gripped the window seal and pushed herself back into the classroom. "What are you doing?"

"Come on, Dorothy. We're busting you out," Jade said.

"But why?" Dorothy asked.

"Duh," Jade said, rolling her eyes. "Because you're innocent. That's why."

"Really, it's okay. I'm fine," Dorothy said, looking back over her shoulder at the door. She expected to see Mr. Macarini return at any moment.

"Look," Gigi said, her hands propped on her round hips. "Your grandma went to a lot of trouble to put that snake in Mr. Macarini's car. And if you don't come NOW, we're all going to get busted."

"Grandma? Snake?!" A ribbon of fear coiled itself around Dorothy's heart and squeezed. Dorothy craned her head through the window and dared a glance at the parking lot. There, idling at the curb, was the long black hearse with a pink lightning bolt on the door. Dead Betty.

But instead of Grandma sitting behind the steering wheel, there was a strange driver with squashed features and unnaturally pink skin. A pink-faced child appeared at the window and waved at Dorothy. Dorothy gasped. She'd recognize that wave anywhere. It was her sister! But why was she so pink and misshapen? Sam bounced up and down and long pink ears sprang up around her face. Dorothy groaned. Nylons. Grandma and Sam were wearing pink panty hose over their heads.

"See!" Dinah said, sticking her head out next to Dorothy's. "I told you there'd be bunny rabbits."

Morti pressed his paws against Sam's window and barked happily. The poor dog was wearing pink nylons, too.

Dee shoved Dorothy and Dinah out of the way and squeezed through the window opening. It was not a pretty sight—similar to watching a live yak birth on the animal channel.

"See ya, suckers," Dee said. She hit the ground running and was soon out of sight.

"You shoulds go, too," Juana said, patting Dorothy's back encouragingly.

Lizzy handed Dorothy her backpack. "Don't worry. We'll devise a logical excuse for your absence."

Dinah hopped up and down excitedly. "Be sure to hug a bunny rabbit for me!"

"And count on us for roller derby!" Ruth said.

Dorothy sighed and reluctantly stuck her head and arms through the window. Gigi and Jade pulled her through, and the three girls ran to the car.

Chapter 13

Gigi climbed into the front passenger seat, and Jade and Dorothy slid in back next to Sam.

Grandma gunned the engine. "I've got the need for speed, my hoagies."

"Homies," Gigi said, fastening her belt buckle.

Grandma shifted the car into gear and raced the hearse toward the exit. She swerved clear of the teacher parking lot, where two animal control vehicles flanked an old VW Beetle.

Dorothy caught a glimpse of Mr. Macarini, his face glistening with beads of sweat as an animal control officer inserted a long stick with pinchers through the window of his car.

Dorothy yanked the panty hose off Morti's head in disgust. "Grandma, I can't believe you put a snake in my teacher's car."

"Ain't no thang," Grandma said, uncovering her own face as soon as they were out of the school grounds.

"No, Grandma. It is a *thang*," Dorothy said. "Mr. Macarini is really scared!"

Grandma chuckled. "Chillax, Dot," she said, swerving the hearse through a series of construction cones like a skier on a slalom course. "You should be giving your G-Dawg some props, yo?"

"G-Dawg?" Dorothy said. This was like arguing with an insane person.

"So, who are you today?" Gigi asked. "The ghetto geezer?"

Grandma laughed. "Fo sho, my ninja."

"Hey!" Gigi said. "I do *not* know what you mean by 'my ninja,' but I'm pretty sure I'm offended."

Dorothy pressed the palms of her hands against her eyeballs until she saw stars. "Sorry, Gigi," she said. "Grandma doesn't mean anything by it. Really. She just thinks she's being cool."

"Thinks?" Grandma asked. "Would a not-cool Grandma have tickets to the big derby game tonight?" Grandma clicked open the glove box and pulled out five tickets.

"Real roller derby?" Gigi said, snatching the tickets.

"For me, too?" Sam asked, grinning like a happy gargoyle through the sheer pink material of her panty hose.

"Yup," Grandma said. "Flatiron Sirens vs. the Radon Rollers. It's at the Thriller Auditorium. You girls in?"

"Definitely," Gigi said. "How about you, Jade? Will your mom let you go?"

Jade's shoulders sagged. "To a derby match? Are you kidding?"

"Wait," Dorothy said, blinking. "Your mom lets you play roller derby but won't let you go to a bout?"

Jade cleared her throat and leaned into Dorothy. "Don't tell your grandma," she whispered, "but my mom thinks I've joined the Cupcake Scouts."

Grandma adjusted the rearview mirror so Jade's face came into view. "Speak up, hon. The cupcake whats?"

Jade blew a strand of hair out of her eyes. "All right.

Jade's Cupcake Scout Badges

Can't be beat!

Meringue Badge

All mixed up

Stirring & Mixing Badge

Preheat 350°

Oven Badge

Sprinkled with love

Sprinkle Badge

All cracked up

Master Egg Cracker Badge

Buttercream!

Frosting Badge

If you must know, I told my mom that I joined the Cupcake Scouts, not a roller derby team."

Dorothy frowned at Jade. "Don't you feel bad about lying to your mom?"

Jade raised an eyebrow. "Why? What did you tell *your* mom?"

Dorothy's gaze dropped to her lap, where Morti was chewing his panty hose into a ratty pink ball. She hadn't told her mom anything. Not even when they talked for a half hour on the phone the night before. Actually, it had been easy—not talking about herself. Mom had been too excited about Nashville, her new country songs, and her "dreamy" boyfriend to even bother asking Dorothy how or what she was doing.

Is hiding the truth as bad as lying? Dorothy wondered. Her stomach twisted with guilt.

Jade took a package of wet wipes out of her messenger bag and began rubbing away the temporary tattoos on her forearm. "In my world, what my mom doesn't know won't hurt her. Besides, she's so protective of me, I'd spend my entire life locked in the house with Mr. Wrinkles if she had her way."

127

"Mr. Wrinkles?" Sam asked.

"My cat," Jade said. She pulled a photo out of the side pocket of her messenger bag and handed it to Dorothy. Sam rolled the panty hose up over her eyes and leaned over to see the tiny photo. It was a picture of a hairless cat with wrinkly, white skin, pink eyes, and big triangle ears.

"Mr. Wrinkles is cool," Gigi said. "But not exactly snuggly."

Jade went to work on her other arm with a new wet wipe. "It's like my mom's afraid I'm going to drop dead or something, like my dad did. But for me, doing nothing feels worse than dying."

Dorothy sighed. She knew exactly what if felt like to be held back by an overprotective parent.

"You're not going to turn me in, are you, Sally?" Jade asked.

"Turn you into what?" Grandma replied with a wink in the rearview mirror.

A relieved smile appeared on Jade's valentine-shaped

face. "I guess I am going to the roller derby game tonight after all."

Dorothy smiled, too, but the sour, guilty feeling sat heavily at the bottom of her stomach like a giant pickled egg.

Chapter 14

The Thriller Auditorium was located on the edge of town. Dorothy grew increasingly nervous as they passed buildings covered with graffiti. Trash skittered down the sidewalks like tumbleweeds, and tattered curtains wriggled their sharp fingers through broken window-panes. Was the auditorium going to be as run-down as the rest of the neighborhood? And if so, what kind of people would be there?

Grandma parked the hearse in a five-minute loading zone right in front of the Thriller, and Dorothy, Sam, Gigi, and Jade climbed out of the car. Grandma locked the car doors from inside and joined the girls on the curb.

"Aren't you worried about parking tickets?" Dorothy asked.

"Nope," Grandma said, patting the roof of the car. "I worry about my Betty."

The inside of the auditorium was large and grand, something between an opera house and a sports stadium. Gigantic chandeliers hung like diamond earrings from the soaring, domed ceiling. Rows and rows of bleacher seats descended toward an expansive, oval-shaped wood floor. Pounding rock music echoed off the walls, making Dorothy's body tingle all the way down to her toes.

While Grandma went to claim their "kick-butt seats," Dorothy, Gigi, Jade, and Sam took a tour of the building

At the back of the auditorium, they found a table piled high with fliers, playbills, and baked goods. The table was manned by a pretty blond girl a year or two older than Dorothy.

Sam picked up a chocolate chip cookie as big as her head. "I can't wait to see real roller derby," she told the blond girl.

"Is this your first time at a bout?" the girl asked, ringing

131

up Sam's cookie. She was wearing a cheerleader uniform with a handwritten name tag that read, "Callous Alice."

Gigi perked the collar of her denim jacket and stuck out her chin. "Actually, we're *on* a derby team, if you must know."

"That's cool," Alice said. "I play with the Cheerbleeders. What's your team name?"

"Uh…" Gigi cleared her throat and looked at Dorothy.

"We're the…" Dorothy started. But the only thing that came to mind was the kissy lip sticker inside her locker. Unfortunately, "Hugs 'n' Kisses" was a pretty lame team name. Then she remembered her run-in with Alex that morning and she had an idea. "Slugs 'n' Hisses?"

"Yeah," Gigi said, giving the table a thump with her fist. "We're like snakes that can punch you in the face."

Dorothy and Jade exchanged concerned looks. Why was Gigi acting so tough?

"Slugs 'n' Hisses, you said?" Alice asked, fishing a clipboard out from under the table. She flipped through a few pages. "Your team isn't on the schedule. Should I add you?"

"Sure," Gigi said. "You do that."

"Great. You're coming into the season late, but we just had a team drop out, so we can fit you right in." Alice took several minutes to write "Slugs 'n' Hisses" on each page of the clipboard.

To pass the time, Dorothy leafed through a pamphlet titled *Down and Derby: How the Game Is Played*. It had a description of derby rules, an explanation of how points were scored, and a diagram of the track and team positions.

When Alice finished writing, she handed Gigi a copy of the schedule. "We have some really good junior teams this year. I hope you're ready."

Gigi crushed the schedule into a ball and tossed it to Jade. "We were born ready."

After they paid for three cookies, two Rice Krispies treats, and a few cupcakes for Jade to take home to her mom, the girls headed back to the bleachers to find Grandma.

"You want to explain why you were so rude to Alice?" Jade asked as the group descended the stairs.

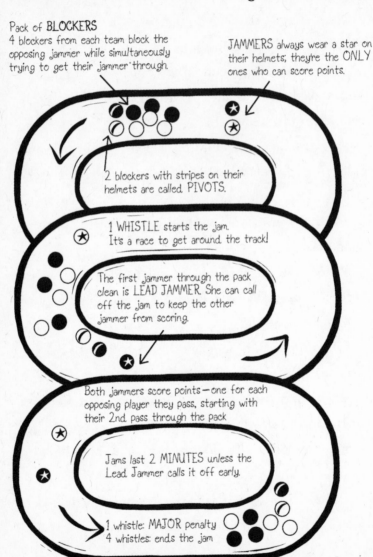

"Me? Rude?" Gigi said. "It was Alice who was all snotty. 'Look at me,'" Gigi mimicked in a high, girly voice. "'I'm blond and pretty and I know everything about roller derby.'"

"I bet we could have learned a lot from her," Dorothy said.

Gigi snorted. "I don't take advice from stuck-up cheerleaders."

"Duh, Gigi," Jade said. "She wasn't a cheerleader. She was a Cheer*bleeder*."

"Whatever. Same thing," Gigi said. "It's over, okay? Let's just watch some roller derby and forget about it."

The girls found Grandma at the bottom of the bleachers. After getting settled and opening their treats, Dorothy only had a couple minutes to look at her *How the Game Is Played* brochure before the music grew louder, announcing the start of the match.

"Jam time!" Grandma hooted. "You girls ready to rock?"

Chapter 15

A tall, thin man in a blazer and bow tie stepped onto the floor and tapped on a microphone.

"Ladies and gentlemen! Girls and boys!" he bellowed in a deep voice. "Please welcome to the track our uncontested national champions, those murderous mermaids of the deep derby sea...the Flatiron Sirens!"

The crowd jumped to its feet, clapped, cheered, and whooped as a dozen skaters raced onto the track. The Sirens wore tattered tutus, fishnet stockings, and sleeveless black T-shirts with their logo on the front—a sharp-toothed mermaid wearing a derby helmet.

A jumbo screen came to life behind the announcer,

and a photo of a grinning woman with long dread-locks appeared.

"First out is a jammer so fast and fierce," the announcer shouted, "she turns her opponents into stone statues. Give it up for...Merdusa!"

The crowd went crazy, stomping loudly on the bleachers as a petite woman shot out of the pack of skaters and waved. Merdusa's thin, pale arms were sleeved in tattoos, and her long dreadlocks flowed out of the back of her starred helmet. Her tiny frame and sweeping strides instantly reminded Dorothy of Jade.

The photo on the screen changed to a heavyset woman with dark brown skin.

"Batten down the hatches, folks, because this next gal is a real loose cannon. Put your hands together for this powerful pivot... Boom-Boom!"

Boom-Boom, wearing a striped helmet, pushed through the pack of skaters and pumped her fist into the air. She thrust her hips to the left and right as the crowd chanted, "Boom, boom! Boom, boom!"

Gigi bumped Dorothy with her hip. "Now that's my kind of derby girl!" she shouted.

As the rest of the Sirens were announced, Dorothy looked and looked for signs of common traits among the players. She couldn't come up with any. Sure, they were all awesome skaters, but they were different sizes and colors and ranged from conservative, librarian types with round-rim glasses and carefully braided ponytails to wild women with shredded fishnet stockings and more piercings and tattoos than the average rock star. Even the skating styles were varied. There were booty-shaking jam dancers like Gigi, speed skaters like Jade, and even one woman who danced and twirled like Alex. Dorothy was beginning to think that her team of oddballs had some potential after all. Maybe you didn't need to be a traditional athlete to be good at roller derby.

After the Sirens had finished a couple of warm-up laps, the Radon Rollers were introduced. Their team was just as mixed as the Sirens. Their jammer was a tall, slender woman named Spinning Jenny. Their pivot, named

Anita Coffee, was a Latin woman with intense eyes who reminded Dorothy of Juana.

Had Juana said she would come to derby practice? Dorothy couldn't remember.

The teams finished their warm-up laps, and several referees rolled onto the floor, taking positions inside and around the edge of the track. Boom-Boom and Anita Coffee, along with three of their teammates, crouched into a ready stance at the starting line. Merdusa and Spinning Jenny rolled into place a few feet behind them. The crowd grew quiet and…

Chapter 16

After the bout, the group returned to Dead Betty to find a small envelope tucked under the windshield wiper.

Dorothy sighed. "It's a parking ticket, isn't it, Grandma?"

"Just a love letter," Grandma said casually, dropping the ticket into her purse. "Your hot granny has a lot of secret admirers, you know."

Gigi harrumphed and climbed into the front passenger seat. "Do all your love letters have police badges printed on the envelope?"

"Only the ones from cops," Grandma said, revving the car engine. "I do love a man in uniform."

As Grandma drove home, Jade fished inside her messenger bag. She pulled out a package of wet wipes and a crumpled ball of paper. She smoothed the paper flat on her lap and yelped.

"Gigi! You loudmouth!"

"What?" Gigi said, turning her head to look at Jade. "I didn't say anything."

Jade shook the paper at her. "Remember this schedule? Do you realize you got us signed up to COMPETE?" She scanned the line-up. "We're supposed to have a bout a week from tonight! Grandma, you have to get us out of this."

Grandma nodded her head slowly back and forth and clicked her tongue. "Sorry, hon. No can do."

JR. ROLLER DERBY

★★ SEASON SCHEDULE ★★

AUGUST 30
MAD GLADISKATERS -vs- CHEERBLEEDERS

SEPTEMBER 6 Slugs 'n' Hisses
PEANUT BUTTER JAMMERS -vs- DOOMSDAY PRINCESSES

SEPTEMBER 13
CRASHTEST HUNNIES -vs- ROLLING ROSES

SEPTEMBER 20
SLUGHERS -vs- CHEERBLEEDERS

SEPTEMBER 27
ROLLING ROSES -vs- PEANUT BUTTER JAMMERS

OCTOBER 3 Slugs 'n' Hisses
MAD GLADISKATERS -vs- DOOMSDAY PRINCESSES

OCTOBER 10
CHEERBLEEDERS -vs- ROLLING ROSES

OCTOBER 17
★ CHAMPIONSHIPS ★

"Why not?" Dorothy felt like she was going to throw up. "We can't compete. I can barely even skate."

Grandma chuckled. "Then I guess you better learn."

"Seriously, G-ma," Gigi said. "Can't you just call someone and get us taken off the bout schedule?"

"Lookie, girls, I may be a little bit of a rule breaker, but I've never missed a game. And I'm not about to now. Besides, there's nothing like an upcoming bout to whip a team into shape."

Dorothy's stomach was really churning now. Why wouldn't Grandma call it off? Competing with so little training was practically suicide.

Grandma caught Dorothy's gaze in the rearview mirror and winked. But instead of making Dorothy feel better, it just made her angry. Really angry.

Fine, then, Dorothy thought, giving Grandma the nastiest look she could muster. *If you're too stubborn to call this stupid bout off, we'll compete. I'll train my butt off this week. And when I end up a pile of ground beef on the track, you'll be sorry.*

Grandma winked again at Dorothy and leaned to

her left…releasing a fart that sounded like a kazoo being played underwater. Everyone stared at the old woman until the rumbling squeal diminished to a final peep. Soon, the awkward silence was replaced by Grandma's giggles.

"Gross!" Dorothy said.

"Ha ha!" Grandma laughed. "I'm sorry, girls. Just trying to lighten things up. You all look so worried. Come on! Roller derby is supposed to be fun."

Sam started to giggle, and Jade and Gigi joined in soon after.

Dorothy struggled to keep a straight face. Finally, the laughter spluttered through her lips and she gave in. She laughed until her cheeks hurt and she had stitches in her sides. The upcoming bout suddenly didn't seem nearly as menacing.

"Nice one, Shotgun Smelly," Gigi laughed. "I hope you can coach as well as you can pass gas."

"I hope so, too," Grandma said. "Otherwise, you girls are toast!"

Chapter 17

Dorothy, Gigi, and Jade spent the entire weekend skating and doing chores for Uncle Enzo. There were toilets to scrub, carpets to steam clean, and buckets of sludgy black carpet water to dump out.

They also practiced skating. Dorothy's balance, speed, and agility had improved, but every new skill she learned brought new opportunities to fall.

Jade taught her how to do crossovers—moving from the outside of the track to the inside of the track and back again. When Dorothy tried the technique, Gigi teased that they should just change the name of the move to crashovers, since that's all Dorothy seemed to be able to do.

Gigi demonstrated stopping techniques. There was a plow stop (pointing toes together in an upside-down V shape), a hockey stop (turning quickly at a 90-degree angle), and a tomahawk stop (whipping around fast and slamming both stoppers down). But the only stop Dorothy managed to do with any real success was the face stop. After Dorothy blacked out twice from nosebleeds, Gigi and Jade decided they should practice falling without getting hurt. They did one-knee falls, two-knee falls, and Superman falls (falling flat on their forearms). They also practiced returning to their feet as quickly as possible.

By the time Monday's practice rolled around, Dorothy was feeling better about her skating skills. And more important, she was confident that if she fell, she wouldn't give herself a major head injury. Progress.

"I'm ready to try the obstacle course now," she told Grandma as they waited for the rest of the team to show up. Galactic Skate was quiet—all except for the snores coming from the old man sitting behind the rocket-shaped rental desk.

"That's nice, dear," Grandma said. "But no obstacle course today."

"But why?" Dorothy asked, disappointed. "You said…"

The front door swung open. In came Gigi, Jade, and Dinah, all chatting and laughing loudly.

Grandma pinched Dorothy's cheek. "That was before you all got yourselves signed up to compete. Friday is going to be here sooner than you think. We need to assign positions and teach everyone the rules."

"Rules?" Gigi said, as the group reached the skate desk. "I thought you didn't care about rules, G-ma."

"I care," Grandma said. "I just like breaking them, too. Anyway, Max is taking over your training tonight. He's better at the technical stuff."

Dorothy blushed. She was embarrassed enough when Max watched her skate from a distance. Now he'd be coaching?

Max rolled up and greeted Grandma with their special handshake. After finishing the zombie robot move, he turned and looked at the girls. "Uh," he said, his eyebrows arched, "you know we can't do roller derby with

148

just four girls." The fluorescent light above him rattled and made a soft, metallic buzzing sound. Dorothy looked around nervously at her teammates.

"Don't worry," Dinah said cheerily. "They'll be here."

Just then, Ruth and Lizzy rolled in through the front door. Ruth was wearing the same oversized T-shirt she had been wearing at school, but Lizzy looked like she was ready for mortal combat. With football pads covered in spikes and scales, the thin girl looked even scrawnier than usual.

She knocked a fist against her armored chest and greeted the team with a salute. "Hail Derbylings! Geekzilla and Rolling Thunder reporting for duty."

Ruth giggled, saluting, too.

Grandma returned the gesture and smiled. "At ease, cadets."

"What's with the costume?" Gigi asked.

"It's not a costume. It's DinoStar battle armor," Lizzy said. "Standard issue."

"This is our standard issue," Jade said, lifting the flap on her messenger bag. She pulled out a stack of black T-shirts and handed them to Lizzy. They had been imprinted with a Slugs 'n' Hisses logo.

"Wow," Dorothy said when the stack was passed to

her. The shirts were amazing. Jade had really outdone herself with the logo design, and they looked professionally printed.

Dorothy selected her T-shirt before handing the remaining shirts back to Jade. Even with the addition of Lizzy and Ruth, the team was still seriously undermanned.

"Too bad Juana didn't come," Dorothy said, pulling the T-shirt on over her clothes. She could do without Dee, but the team could really use Juana. Her intensity and thoughtfulness would be a great addition. If only she could get over being so shy.

Dorothy looked up to see the rest of her team grinning at her. She felt a soft tap on the shoulder.

"Sorry to be lates," said a soft voice.

Dorothy whirled around and smiled at Juana. "You came!"

Juana nodded. Her long, dark hair was pulled back in a ponytail. "I'm ready to be braves, Dorty!"

Dorothy gave Juana a big hug.

"Okay, well, you are going to need more people to make an official team," Max said, "but let's get practicing.

151

Our first bout is this Friday, and we don't have a minute to waste."

Grandma wished everyone luck and took Sam with her to run some errands.

Dorothy and her team strapped on their pads and helmets and rolled to the rink floor. An oval track had been marked off with white tape.

"Time trials, people. Trust me, you'll need the endurance," Max announced. "Line up!"

When Max blew his whistle, Jade and Gigi zipped out in front of the others. Jade pulled ahead at the first turn, but Gigi rushed forward and cut Jade off. Jade juked to the inside of the track to pass Gigi again, but Gigi swung her hip and bumped Jade so hard that she tumbled into the center of the rink.

Max blew his whistle.

"No hits during time trials, girls. That means you, Gigi. Keep that vicious booty under control!"

"Aw!" Gigi said. "But Booty Vicious is my middle name."

"I thought Eleanor was your middle name," Jade growled, dusting herself off and returning to the track.

Gigi shrugged. "I guess Booty Vicious will just have to be my skate name, then."

Max called everyone back to the starting line and restarted his stopwatch.

On the second trial, Jade came in first and Gigi was second. Rolling Thunder had been in third, but crashed into a wall just short of the finish line, so Juana came in before her. Geekzilla came in fifth after Rolling Thunder, and Dorothy and Dinah came in dead last.

Dorothy rolled to a stop several feet away from her team and pounded her head against the top of the wall. Even with all her extra training, she wasn't any faster than the goofiest, least focused member of the team. It was plain embarrassing.

"Hey, Undead!" Dinah shouted. "Look who's here!"

Dorothy didn't look up. It would just be Alex, wanting to take over the skate floor as usual.

Suddenly, two meaty hands shot out of nowhere and picked Dorothy up by the shirt, wrenching her up so she was face-to-face with the beast from detention.

Dee.

Chapter 18

"Hey twerp," Dee grunted.

Dorothy shrieked and tried to wrestle free.

Juana appeared at the wall. "Dee! You puts Dorty down!"

"Why?" Dee said with a chuckle. "You wanna smack her for me?"

Juana scrunched her eyebrows, confused.

After a moment she nodded. "Yes. I am Juana SmackHer. Now you lets her go!"

"Suit yourself," Dee said, and dropped Dorothy so hard that her teeth rattled.

"You are okay?" Juana checked.

"I am now," Dorothy said. "Thanks to Juana SmackHer."

Juana grinned.

"Huh," Dee said, looking from Dorothy to Juana. "I came down here thinking you all were gonna be a bunch of babies. But if this team is tough enough to make a wimp like Juana stand up to me, then it's a good enough team for Dee Tension."

"Dee Tension?" Dorothy said, glaring up at the brute. She was still furious. "*That's* your skate name?"

"Why?" Dee growled, reaching over the wall and placing two thick hands on Dorothy's shoulders. "You got somethin' better, twerp?"

Sure, Dorothy thought. *Dee Lusional, Dee Mented, Dee Sgusting...*But something told her that she was better off keeping those ideas to herself.

Dorothy wriggled out of Dee's hold. "Um, no. On second thought, that's actually a great name for you. Very clever."

Dee slicked her hair back and chuckled. "I know, huh? Now let's roller derby!"

The fluorescent light above Dee sizzled and went dead. Chills ran up Dorothy's spine.

Max rolled over and proceeded to explain to the massive girl why picking on fellow team members wouldn't be tolerated.

Dorothy took the opportunity to slink back to the rest of her team. She was feeling seriously shaken. Between Dee and Eva, things were getting out of hand. How could anyone be expected to concentrate in these conditions?

Once Dee was geared up, Max assigned positions. Jade was the obvious choice for jammer, and Gigi claimed the pivot position. Dorothy silently hoped Gigi's bossiness would make her a good leader, but she had her concerns. The rest of the girls were blockers.

"And we'll need at least one backup jammer," Max said.

Jade grabbed Dorothy's hand and raised it. "Dorothy volunteers."

"I do?" Dorothy said. Was Jade kidding? She had just tied Dinah for slowest skater on the team. Definitely not jammer material.

"Don't worry, Dorothy," Jade whispered. "I'm not going to need any backup. I can handle this on my own."

Dorothy was confused. Did Jade really want to keep

156

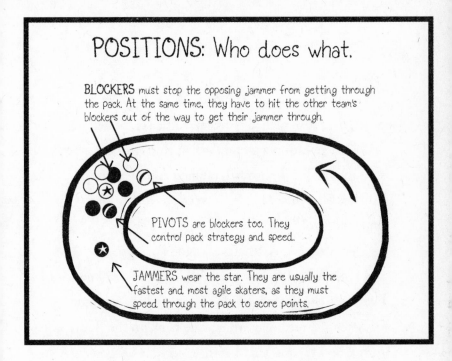

POSITIONS: Who does what.

BLOCKERS must stop the opposing jammer from getting through the pack. At the same time, they have to hit the other team's blockers out of the way to get their jammer through.

PIVOTS are blockers too. They control pack strategy and speed.

JAMMERS wear the star. They are usually the fastest and most agile skaters, as they must speed through the pack to score points.

the jammer position all to herself? Before Dorothy could open her mouth to refuse, Max smiled his lopsided grin and put a star cover over her helmet.

Moments later they were deep into the next exercise: arm whips. It felt exhilarating to be rocketed into hyper speed. Everyone was laughing and having a great time whipping and being whipped, right up until Dee and Ruth's turn.

"Take it easy," Max warned as Dee held out her massive arm.

Rolling Thunder grabbed Dee's arm only to be launched with such force that Ruth scraped along the wall like cheese on a grater. When Ruth finally came to a stop, her right thigh was scratched and bleeding.

Max blew his whistle. "Excessive force, Dee. Get it under control."

Dee shrugged. "Whatever, dude."

Dorothy had to put her head between her knees and take deep breaths while Max bandaged the wound.

After a short break, they were back on the floor. The next exercise was skating in a pack. The goal was to keep in tight formation and skate at the same speed. Dorothy's team looked less like a pack and more like a group of confused geriatrics lost at the mall. To fix the problem, Max found some rope and tied the girls together elbow to elbow. In theory, this was an okay idea. In reality, it was a disaster. If one person fell, everyone fell. If one person skated a little faster than the pack, everyone fell. Basically, if anyone did anything, everyone fell. Bruised and battered, the girls begged Max to untie them.

"So what brilliant exercise do you have planned now?" Gigi grumbled once she was finally free. "You could fill the rink with live alligators."

"Or baby otters!" Dinah suggested.

"Or baby otters and alligators," Jade said, a wicked glint in her eye.

"How about we just sit down and discuss the rules of roller derby," Max said. The lights flickered, but no one seemed to notice except Dorothy.

Fifteen minutes later, everyone was more confused about the rules than they had been before the discussion started. Dorothy's head hurt like she had just finished a snow-cone-eating contest. Even Geekzilla, the smartest girl on the team, looked completely lost.

"How about we just try a practice game?" Dorothy suggested.

"What's the point?" Gigi grumbled.

"Agreed," Jade said. "If we don't understand the rules now…"

"No," Juana said. "Dorty is right. We will learns better by doing, no?"

Dorothy smiled at Juana. At least one person on the team thought her ideas had value.

"All right, Dorth," Max said. "Let's do it your way. Jam time!"

Two jams later, Dorothy still hadn't passed an opposing blocker, so she hadn't scored a single point, but she didn't care. The idea had paid off, and the Slugs 'n' Hisses were playing real roller derby.

When Alex did finally arrive at Galactic Skate, she commandeered the center of the rink. Alex's swirling, twirling, and leaping made it hard to concentrate on the game. Why did Alex have to show off like that? Was she intentionally trying to distract them?

To make matters worse, every time Jade broke through the pack and raced around the rink, Alex would roll up alongside her, skating faster backward than Jade could manage forward.

"Stop it, Alex!" Jade yelled. "Back away from the track!"

"I'm just practicing," Alex said.

had been spread

multiple penaltie

didn't notice or sl

"Every girl for

"Team sport, h

Gigi made a d

any of Geekzilla's

"That is affirm

playbook. "I failed

able. Dinah, woul

a seizure in the mi

"That wasn't a

appeared to be vib

"That was the Ho

wiggling her botto

like an injured duc

If that was the F

had never seen bef

"Well, it is kind

team," Dorothy

Unfortunately, Din

"Practice somewhere else!" Jade yelled. "The track is roller derby only!"

Just as Jade said the words "roller derby" there was a thunderous sound of cracking wood, like a tree splitting in two, followed by a heart-freezing shriek. Dorothy's eyes darted desperately around the track in search of the source of the wails. When she found it, she let out a shriek of her own. The track floor was eating Rolling Thunder! The big girl had already been swallowed up to her waist and the rink was hungrily consuming her top half an inch at a time.

Dorothy rushed to the hole and grabbed one of Ruth's flailing arms, while Jade grabbed the other and pulled. As hard as they tugged, they couldn't free the howling girl from the jaws of the hungry floor.

"Let me," Dee said, grabbing a fistful of Ruth's T-shirt. With one mighty yank, Dee pulled Rolling Thunder clean out of the hole. To Dorothy's relief, the bottom half of the big girl was still intact.

Dorothy bent over Ruth. "Are you okay?"

Ruth giggled softly and nodded, but looked terrified.

By this time everyone had arrived at the edge of the

G
ar
fe
w

G
in
Sl
h
M
cl
cl

fo
sp
w
h
w
g

a
st
st

a

of

di

he
m

(B

to

we

ca

really bee
much big
Jade fr
against th
"Yeah,
"Kind of
the roller
"Beatir
either," D
"Uh, le
gested. "M
Lizzy t
probably n
"Don't
tall girl or
can hurt y

Twenty minute
"Well, that
team shuffled
"You're tel
sore behind.
"I blame my
more attention
Grandma said,
in her pocket. "
"I like your s
Grandma tu
"That's why I d
"It's not you
face and arms w
Strawberry Shor
Dorothy nod
our lives."
"Perhaps if G
and pacing," Li
blockers must sta
Dorothy sighe

too. What was worse, one of Dinah's crazy kicks had collided with Dorothy's skate, and their wheels had become linked. They couldn't pull their feet apart and ended up tripping one of the Peanuts. Both Dorothy and Dinah went to the penalty box for that mishap.

What Slugs 'n' Hisses needs is some creative coaching, Dorothy thought. *Why doesn't Grandma make Gigi skate backward? Then Gigi would have to look at the pack.*

Dorothy's thoughts were interrupted by a tug on her shirt. It was Juana. "You are thinking something, no? You shoulds tell us."

Dorothy sighed and shook her head. "No. Just a dumb idea. No one would listen to me, anyway."

"I woulds," Juana said.

Dorothy looked at Juana. The dark-haired girl looked so sincere.

"Well," Dorothy said, "I was just thinking that Gigi could skate backward, and…" She was about to add that Jade should pass the star occasionally. Jade was good, but she got so winded she had to call time-outs just to catch her breath.

"Skate backward?" Gigi snorted. "No offense, Undead, but that is a dumb idea."

Dorothy's confidence deflated like a punctured tire. "Oh," she said, her shoulders sagging. *So much for speaking up.*

Still, the Slugs had to make improvements, and soon. If they continued to botch games like this, they were sure to lose, or worse, injure players. Nobody wanted to be on a team that lost all the time. Including Dorothy. But what could she do?

Chapter 20

Over the next six weeks, Dorothy's team practiced every day after school. Grandma's no-nonsense coaching was working. The pack was tighter, and Dorothy's speed was better. Dinah's goofiness was in check, and Rolling Thunder hardly ever crashed now.

Still, no amount of coaching could cure Gigi from getting in Jade's way—and no amount of exhaustion would convince Jade that she needed to share her jamming duties.

Despite all that, the Slugs 'n' Hisses had won their last three games!

Their first victory came when the Rolling Roses never showed up at the bout.

Their second win was against the unbeaten SlugHERS. The SlugHERS lost by one point, blaming the loss on their absent pivot, Quaranteen, who was home in bed with the chicken pox.

The Slugs' most recent victory was against the Crash Test Hunnies. It had been a close game, but Dorothy's team had been able to shut out the Hunnies' jammer, Knocks Zeema, and give Jade just the opening she needed to score an extra five points for the win.

The last game of the season was one week before Halloween. The Slugs were scheduled to battle the Doomsday Princesses. The bout took place at the Grossman Rec Center, almost an hour's drive west into the mountains. It had started snowing earlier that day—the first snow of the season—and Dead Betty had fishtailed the entire drive. Dorothy was already on her last nerve by the time they pulled into the rec center parking lot.

The inside of the center smelled like a Mt. Everest of dirty gym socks. Dorothy's eyes watered from the stench, but through the blur she saw a familiar face.

"Max!" she cried, and ran to greet him at the check-in desk.

He opened his arms and she almost hugged him, but thought better of it and offered a hand instead.

Max shook it and gave her a lopsided grin.

"What are you doing here?" Gigi asked.

"Guess," Max said, taking off his jacket. Underneath was a black-and-white shirt.

Dorothy's heart skipped a beat. "You're a referee?"

"And guess what else?" he said, his eyes twinkling. "I've been looking at the lineup, and if you win this game, you're in the championship bout!"

Grandma gave Max a high five while the girls exchanged confused looks.

"But that's statistically impossible," Geekzilla said. "The Slugs have only won three games."

"Well," Max said. "Since you guys replaced another team, your averages are still great. Win tonight, and you play the Cheerbleeders on Halloween night."

He gestured for everyone to follow him to the basketball courts. The back of his jersey said Max Voltage.

The court was as disappointing as the rest of the building. The floor was worn and cracked, and had been repaired in spots with duct tape. It also looked like it hadn't been mopped in at least a decade.

"Any luck talking Uncle Enzo into letting us have our bouts at Galactic Skate?" Dorothy asked.

Max sighed and draped an arm over Dorothy's shoulder. "Actually, I was going to tell you after the game, but I might as well break it to you now."

"Oh no," Dorothy said. "Galactic Skate isn't closing, is it?" Where would they skate? Where would Alex skate…and since when did she care about Alex?

Max's serious face cracked into a grin. "No, Dorth. Actually, if Slugs 'n' Hisses wins tonight, Uncle Enzo agreed to hold the championship bout at Galactic Skate!"

"Really?" Dorothy said, and she threw her arms around Max's waist.

Dorothy's team jumped up and down and cheered.

"Yup," he said, squeezing back. He smelled good, like oranges and cinnamon. Suddenly Dorothy felt everyone's eyes on her and she let go.

"But you have to win this bout first, okay?" he said with a wink.

Dorothy's cheeks felt hot.

Grandma cleared her throat. "Hey. Max Voltage. You better skedaddle before the other team catches you getting all hoochie coochie with the enemy."

Dorothy shot Grandma a menacing look. *Hoochie coochie?*

Max raised his eyebrows flirtatiously and skated away.

Rolling Thunder and Dinah giggled until Dorothy shot them a disapproving look. They stopped for a minute, but started giggling again after Dinah made kissy noises.

"So," Lizzy said. "I've been developing some new plays." She handed out a sheet of paper to everyone on the team. "I made some observations at the Doomsday Princesses' last bout, and I have identified a few weaknesses we can exploit."

"You spied on the Princesses?" Gigi asked, looking impressed.

Lizzy smiled and pushed her glasses up her nose. "I prefer the term 'field research.'"

Dorothy looked at the paper and suddenly felt very hopeful. These plays might actually work! "Nice 'field research,' Geekzilla. We might actually get to that championship game after all!"

Thanks to Lizzy, the team was finally working together, and...

LIZZY'S PLAY #1, SPLIT ENDS: PUSH POWER! GEEKZILLA SUPPORTS RED WHILE SHE GIVES THUNDER A GIANT PUSH INTO RUFFPUNZEL. BAM!

LIZZY'S PLAY #2, THE POISON APPLE: GEEKZILLA, BOOTY VICIOUS, AND JUANA GIVE SNOW WHITE KNUCKLES A "BAD" APPLE 3-WAY BLOCK.

LIZZY'S PLAY #3, BIPPITY BOPPITY BOOM: BOOTY VICIOUS STRIKES AGAIN! GIGI'S GIANT HIP BLOCK SENDS CINDERHELLIAN SPINNING.

WE'RE GOING TO THE CHAMPIONSHIPS!!!

Chapter 21

"Let's go," Grandma said, tucking her spiky pink hair into a nun's habit. "We're running late. Don't want to miss your big championship game!"

Halloween had arrived sunny but cold. The Night of the Rolling Dead was tonight, and Dorothy was in her uniform: her Slugs 'n' Hisses T-shirt and a skirt. She'd used eye shadow to apply a dark circle around one eye and a dark line under the other for dramatic effect. For a final touch, she'd used Grandma's red lipstick to paint blood dripping from the corners of her mouth. It had made her queasy to look at herself in the mirror, but she definitely looked like an Undead Redhead now.

Grandma was dressed as the Shotgun Nun. Her outfit was mostly a nun costume, except Grandma had shortened the dress so it just barely covered her behind. "All the better to show off my new fishnets and thigh-high boots," she had said.

"Let's do this," Dorothy said, feeling a sudden rush of excitement about the big game. She headed to the door, picked up her skates by the laces, and yanked the door open.

There stood her mother, one hand raised, ready to knock.

"Trick or treat!" she said, wrapping her arms around her startled daughter.

Dorothy swallowed hard. Was this a dream? Mom? Here at Grandma's house? Remembering the forbidden skates in her hand, she carefully shifted them so they were concealed behind her back.

Sam ran up and hugged Mom. Sam was wearing the Slugs 'n' Hisses Official Cheerleader T-shirt Jade had made for her.

"Are you surprised to see me?" Mom asked, holding Sam out at arm's length. Mom's hair was now platinum blond instead of red. Her smile was bleach white.

"Uh, very surprised," Dorothy said. She bit her bottom lip. "So, why didn't you call?"

Mom grinned. "And ruin all the fun?"

"Are you here to take us to Nashville?" Sam said, bouncing up and down.

Mom laughed and tucked a loose strand of curly hair behind Sam's ear. "No, Samantha. Just visiting. I thought I'd stop in on my way to California. Nashville really isn't working out for Mommy, so I'm going to L.A. to become an actress. Isn't that cool? Your mom, a Hollywood star!"

"But you're gonna take us with you, right?" Sam said, clutching Mom's jacket sleeve.

"Come on, Sammy. Don't be like that," Mom said, peeling Sam's fingers off her arm and smoothing out the wrinkled suede. "L.A. isn't any good for kids. Smoggy, lots of traffic. Besides, I'm going to be really busy with auditions and movie shoots and things. You understand, don't you, honey?"

Tears pooled in the little girl's eyes.

Dorothy wrapped a protective arm around her little sister's shoulder. "Why did you even come here?"

Mom furrowed her brow. "Dorothy Anne Moore. What's gotten into you? I thought you'd be happy to see me." Her eyes assessed her daughter critically. "So," she said, suspiciously, "what's with the makeup and clothes? Don't tell me you've gone all goth on us."

Dorothy shook her head. "Uh...just a Halloween costume."

Mom's look turned angry. "And this?" she said, pushing a fake fingernail into the Slugs 'n' Hisses logo on Dorothy's T-shirt. "Is this for Halloween, too?"

"Mom!" Dorothy said, shifting away, but her skate wheels clacked together behind her back.

"Ah-ha!" Mom said, reaching behind Dorothy's back to pull the skates out of Dorothy's hand. She held them up in the air like a detective who had just found the murder weapon.

Mom's eyes shifted to Grandma, who was now standing at the foot of the stairs. "You did this," she growled. "You got my girls into roller derby, didn't you?"

"But, Mom," Sam said. "Roller derby is awesome. And Dorothy is really good. She's in the championship bout tonight. You should come!"

"A derby bout?" Mom said, furious. She paced in front of the door like a caged panther. "Did it ever occur to you *why* I forbade you to roller-skate?"

Because you're a control freak? Dorothy thought angrily.

"Because roller derby ruined my childhood," Mom said, still pacing. "Other girls had normal moms. Moms who baked cookies, tucked them in at night, showed up to parent-teacher conferences and dentist appointments. And what did I have?" She planted her feet and shook the skates at Grandma. "Shotgun Sally! A woman too busy gallivanting around the country with her team to bother being there for *me*." Mom lowered her head and her shoulders trembled.

"Oh, Dolly," Grandma said, her high-heel boots clacking on the tile floor as she walked to her daughter, arms open.

Mom's head shot up, and she held her hand out like a crossing guard. "Don't call me that!" she snarled. "I'm not your Dolly anymore. I'm Holly now." Mom wiped tears from her eyes and looked at Dorothy and Sam. Her voice was sweet again. "Don't you like it, girls? I haven't decided on a last name yet. I'm thinking about Wood, or Jolly, or Mackerel. You know, something with star power."

Dorothy stared at her mom, dumbstruck. Holly Mackerel? Really? Dorothy was beginning to think Mom was crazier than Grandma. At least Grandma was fun crazy. Supportive and encouraging crazy. Sure, Grandma drove too fast and broke just about every parking law in existence, but she had their back, too. Mom only seemed to be worried about one person. Herself.

"We really have to go now," Dorothy said, reaching for the skates. She didn't want to talk anymore. She was too angry. "My team is waiting."

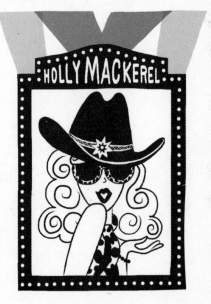

Mom planted her feet in front of the door and held the skates out of reach. "No! Roller derby took my mom away from me. I will not let it take my children, too!"

"Take *us* away?" Dorothy spat. It was all she could do to keep herself from body slamming her mom. "It's you who went away. Not us."

"What did you say?" Mom's voice was thin, like all the air had been sucked out of the room.

Dorothy's heart thudded in her chest. She had never talked back to Mom before. She gritted her teeth and strained to keep her voice calm and even. "I haven't noticed you tucking us in at night. Or baking us cookies or coming to parent-teacher conferences."

Mom's eyes widened with shock and hurt. "But that's different." She hesitated. "I'm different. It's not like I'm playing stupid roller derby. I'm building a serious career, following my dreams. Didn't you hear, Dorothy? I'm going to be a star!"

Right. Totally different, Dorothy thought.

"Okay," Dorothy said flatly. "You go be a star. Send us a postcard or something." She reached her hands out for the skates. "Now if you don't mind, I have a stupid roller derby championship to win."

"Fine," Mom said, defeated, dropping the skates at Dorothy's feet.

Dorothy barely managed to hop out of the way before the skates hit her toes.

Mom shook her head at Dorothy. "I always did think you took after your grandmother. Feisty. Rebellious. I did my best to tame you, but I see now that it was a lost cause."

She turned on her heel. "I wish I had never come here," she mumbled, then slammed the door so hard that the furniture jumped.

"That makes two of us," Dorothy said to the door.

Sam burst into tears and flung her arms around Dorothy's waist.

Dorothy sighed and held her sister tightly. She immediately regretted arguing with Mom. She should have bit her tongue, at least for Sam's sake.

Grandma tutted softly and wrapped both girls in her strong arms. "She'll come around, you'll see. She may have changed her name, her hair color, and her address, but she's still your mom and she loves you. She just needs some time to find herself. She'll be back."

"Really?" Sam snuffled.

"Sure," Grandma said. "I promise."

Just then there was a loud knock at the door.

"Mom?" Sam said, rushing to open it.

But it wasn't Mom. It was two police officers in dark uniforms, displaying shiny silver badges.

Chapter 22

"Sally Kilpatrick?" one of the officers said, scrutinizing Grandma.

"That depends," Grandma said, pulling at the hem of her short skirt.

"You're the driver in this photograph, aren't you?" the other officer said, holding up a photo radar ticket.

"And you want my autograph?" Grandma said, batting her eyes.

The officers did not look amused. "No, ma'am. We have a warrant for your arrest. Seems you have a few outstanding tickets to take care of."

"You mean the love letters?" Sam asked.

"Yes, honey," Grandma said. "The love letters. These are Grandma's boyfriends. Nothing to worry about."

One of the police officers turned to Dorothy. "Do you have another parent or guardian on the premises? Or will you be coming to the station with us?"

"Their mom is just around the corner," Grandma said quickly. "You're going to a roller derby bout, aren't you, girls?"

Dorothy and Sam looked at each other and nodded. Technically, that was all true.

"We never miss a bout!" Grandma handed her duffel bag and keys to Dorothy. "I'll meet up with you after my date with these two handsome officers, okay?"

Dorothy and Sam watched helplessly as Grandma, still wearing her ridiculous nun costume, was handcuffed and escorted into the back of the police car. They were completely alone now.

"How does Grandma expect us to get to Galactic Skate?" Dorothy

192

wondered out loud. She looked down at the duffel bag and then at the car keys.

"Dead Betty!" Sam yelled. Both girls raced to the driveway, where the gleaming hearse waited like the magic carriage in a fairy tale.

Once inside, Dorothy slipped the key into the ignition. A sudden wave of nervousness washed over her. Maybe this wasn't such a good idea. She could barely even see over the steering wheel. "Maybe we should just call Gigi or Jade or something."

"They're already at the bout," Sam said. "It starts in less than twenty minutes. Come on, Dorothy. You can do it!"

Dorothy sucked in a deep breath. Mom had called her "feisty" and "rebellious," and she was about to prove her right. "Okay. Here goes nothing." Dorothy twisted the car key and the hearse roared to life. She yanked the stick shift into reverse and tapped the gas pedal with a toe. The engine purred but the car didn't move. Dorothy scooted forward in her seat and pressed her whole foot down on the pedal. With a deafening roar, Dead Betty rocketed backward down the driveway…and smashed into the mailbox with a metallic crunch.

Dorothy and Sam were thrown back against their seats and flung forward toward the dashboard. Luckily, they were both wearing seat belts. The restraints bit into Dorothy's shoulder and waist, but neither she nor Sam was injured. Dorothy and Sam jumped out of the coughing, sputtering hearse to survey the damage.

Dorothy's stomach lurched. The rear bumper was twisted around the ornate cement mailbox post. Black smoke poured out of the exhaust pipe. Dead Betty wasn't going anywhere now.

"Frappit, frappit, frappit!" Dorothy shouted. "I knew this was a bad idea. Grandma is going to kill us!"

"And how are we going to get to the bout?" Sam said sadly.

Dorothy shook her head. "We're not." She sat down on the curb. The sky had turned dark, and streetlights were casting yellow pools on the pavement. Somewhere nearby, kids were calling, "trick or treat!"

"Come on, Dorothy. We can't let the team down," Sam said. "The Slugs don't have a chance without you."

Dorothy's body felt wasted—drained of energy. Like she had been sucked dry by those closet vampires after all. All she wanted to do now was close her eyes and never open them again. "It's all over, Sam. I give up. Slugs 'n' Hisses loses."

"Don't give up," Sam said, sitting down next to Dorothy and placing a hand on her sister's knee. "I believe in you."

Dorothy shook her head. Her sister meant well, but they were completely out of options now. It would take at least an hour to skate to the bout, and even if they had money for a taxi, they couldn't hail one from the mortuary driveway.

"Hey, look," Sam said, pointing at a silver Lexus sedan that was headed up their street. "Isn't that…?"

Dorothy squinted. As the sedan passed under a street lamp, Dorothy saw someone looking out of the backseat window. Someone with a silky blond ponytail rippling in the breeze.

Chapter 23

Dorothy and Sam leapt to their feet and waved their arms like two castaways who had just spotted a rescue plane. Dorothy never imagined she'd actually be excited to see Alex.

The Lexus glided to a stop in front of the funeral home.

Alex wrinkled her nose. "Aren't you supposed to be at Galactic Skate?"

"Well, we…" Dorothy said, nodding toward the wrecked hearse, "don't have a ride."

The front passenger-side window rolled down and a handsome man with highlights said, "You do now! We were just headed there."

Alex's face blanched.

"The door, Alexandra?"

"Uh…it's a short walk," Alex offered brightly. After getting a stern look from her dad, Alex sighed, opened her door, and scooted over. The trunk door clicked open and Dorothy threw her duffel bag in back, then joined Sam inside the car.

"Uh, hi," Alex said.

The two men in the front seat turned and smiled at Dorothy and her sister.

"Come on, Alex," the man in the passenger seat prodded. "Aren't you going to introduce us?"

"These are, um…" Alex shifted uncomfortably.

The attractive dark-haired man in the driver's seat put the car in drive. "Give her a minute, Jerry. You know she's sensitive about us."

Jerry shook his head. "All right, David. But seriously, I'm just tired of her trying to pass us off as her bodyguards or pool boys or whatever she's calling us these days. It's the twenty-first century. Why can't she just tell the truth?"

"Fine," Alex said, her eyes dropping to her manicured nails. Her voice was barely audible. "These are my...dads."

"Hooray!" The man in the passenger seat said. "Did you hear that, David? She claimed us!"

"Now that wasn't so hard, was it?" David said.

"You have two dads?" Sam asked, impressed. "We don't even have one."

"We have a dad," Dorothy said. "We just don't ever see him."

Dorothy held out her hand to the dad in the passenger seat. "I'm Dorothy, by the way. And this is Samantha."

"I'm Jerry," he said, shaking Dorothy's hand, "and this is my husband, David."

"Now hold up," David said, tilting his head to look at Dorothy. "You're not *the* Dorothy who's using Jerry's old locker, are you?"

"Locker #13?" Jerry asked excitedly.

Dorothy glared at Alex. Alex bit her lip. Now Dorothy knew why she had been so touchy about her locker.

"So how's my Mr. Pretty Penguin holding up?" Jerry asked.

"Uh, he's good, I guess," Dorothy said, not breaking eye contact with Alex. "Although he has some new lines on his face."

Alex blushed.

"Don't we all," David said with a laugh.

Jerry sighed. "Ah, Mr. Pretty. I've always had a thing for beauty pageants. The dresses, the hair, the makeup. Did you know that Alex won forty-six crowns when she was little?"

"Really?" Sam said.

"You're embarrassing me, Daddy," Alex said.

"Okay, okay, I'll stop," Jerry said. "But you know those were some of my proudest moments. I designed all her costumes. Broke my heart when she said she wanted to do artistic skating instead of pageants. But when Alex sets her mind to something…"

Alex huffed. "You still get to make all my outfits."

"I know, I know. But it's all medals and trophies now. I miss the crowns and sashes, honey."

"I don't," Alex grumbled.

"Uh, so why are you guys going to my roller derby bout?" Dorothy asked suspiciously.

"What?" David said. "Don't tell me you didn't tell them that, either, Alexandra."

"It was going to be a *surprise*, Dad," Alex said.

"What kind of surprise?" Dorothy asked. She wasn't sure if she wanted any more surprises from Alex.

"A fabulous one," Jerry said.

"Just something I wanted you and the Pompoms to see," Alex said.

Dorothy choked. "What? The Pompoms? They're coming?" Dorothy could just imagine Alex ordering the Pompoms onto the track to ambush her team mid-bout. Isn't that what she'd done that first night at the roller rink?

Dorothy narrowed her eyes at Alex. "And I suppose you invited your evil roller ballerina friends, too?"

Alex looked puzzled.

"You know," Dorothy said, "those high school roller skaters at Galactic Skate—the ones you sent to attack us?"

"My teammates? No. I didn't invite them. And they

aren't my friends, either. Frienemies, maybe. And I've never sent them to do anything."

"What?" Dorothy couldn't believe that Alex was denying her part in that attack. "Then why did you point at me and—" Dorothy ran her finger across her throat like a knife. "Next thing we knew you were gone and your teammates were all over us." Dorothy shuddered involuntarily as the whole terrible scene replayed in her mind.

Alex looked shocked. "But I...I wasn't telling them to attack you. Honest. I was just explaining what the Pompoms would do to *me* if they found out I was a skater. That's why I left Galactic Skate so quickly. I didn't want you or Jade or Gigi to see me roller-skate. I was hoping to find somewhere else to practice, but my dads made me go back the next day."

Dorothy shook her head, not quite believing Alex. "So your teammates attacked us...just because?"

"Look, I'm really sorry if they were mean, but they're not nice people, okay?"

Dorothy rubbed the back of her neck. "I want to believe you, but none of this makes any sense. For one, why would the Pompoms even care if you skate? They practically worship you, remember?"

"Maybe. But they despise roller-skating, too, *remember*? I didn't want them to know the truth. 'Alexandra Bijou, the sequin-wearing artistic roller skater with two dads.' Does any of that sound normal to you?"

Dorothy shrugged. "Normal is overrated."

"Amen, sister!" Jerry called from the front seat.

David chuckled.

"Look," Alex continued, "I never meant to hurt you. I just wanted to blend in, okay? And you show up in that sequined gym suit…It was like you were putting a spotlight on all the things I had worked so hard…" she glanced toward her dads in the front seat, "…so hard to hide."

Dorothy sighed. She didn't like it, but Alex's explanation made sense. With the exception of one detail. "So, if you didn't want to hurt me, why did you trip me in the cafeteria?"

Alex shook her head. "Come on, Dorothy. Think about it. That wasn't me. Why would I go out of my way to bring attention to you?"

"Uh…" Dorothy couldn't think of a good answer to that. Finally she nodded. "I'm sorry I blamed you, Alex."

Alex nodded back and looked out the window. "I'm just so sick of the Pompoms. All the stupid projects. The attitudes. But most of all, I'm tired of pretending to be something I'm not."

"And who are you, really?" Dorothy asked.

Alex sighed. "Come on, Dorothy. You already know the answer. I'm a big dork. A weirdo just like you."

Chapter 24

In the fifteen minutes it had taken to drive to Galactic Skate, the sky had grown black. Storm clouds obscured the pale, round face of the Halloween moon.

Dorothy thanked Alex's dads for the ride and raced inside the building with Sam at her heels.

Uncle Enzo was selling tickets at the entrance door. He was grinning like a fox as he stuffed bills into an already overflowing cash box. The wrinkled old man from the skate rental desk stood at his shoulder, shaking his head sadly.

"I'm begging you, son," the old man said. His voice creaked like rusty door hinges. "Call it off now, while you still can."

Dorothy slowed, alarmed by the warning. Was the wrinkly guy asking Enzo to cancel the bout?

"Leave me be, Pops," Enzo said, slamming the lid of the cash box. "I know it's a gamble, but we're just going to have to trust that the old curse is gone now. It's been thirty years already."

"Thirty years tonight," the old man said darkly. Just then, a thunderclap burst outside the building and the lights flickered. Both men looked up. "Trust my words, son," the old man said. "No good will come of this."

Dorothy grabbed Sam's hand and raced down the hallway. The conversation had spooked her, and the sooner she found her teammates the better. Was there really a chance that Eva would take her revenge tonight? Grandma hadn't seemed worried about the bout. But then again, Grandma wasn't here now, either. Why had Grandma had to go and get herself arrested?

Come on, Dorothy. It's just a ghost story. Pull yourself together.

When they reached the rink, Dorothy did a double take. The dirty carpet walls were gone, replaced by tall metal bleachers. The wood floor was polished to a glossy sheen, and the track lines looked professionally painted. Uncle Enzo had really gone all out to get Galactic Skate ready for tonight's bout. And it appeared to be paying off. The bleachers were packed with noisy spectators, most of whom were wearing Halloween costumes. There were superheroes and monsters, witches and pumpkins—even a six-foot banana. Dorothy recognized several faces in the crowd. Merdusa and Boom-Boom from the Flatiron Sirens, kids from school. She even spotted a couple of faculty members.

"Dorothy!" called a friendly voice. It was Mr. Macarini waving to her from halfway up the stands. He was dressed in a beige animal control officer uniform and had what appeared to be a snake wrapped around his neck.

Dorothy jumped involuntarily at the sight of the big snake.

"Gotcha!" Mr. Macarini said with a laugh. He peeled the snake off his neck and shook it. "Rubber!"

Dorothy breathed a sigh of relief and gave the teacher a thumbs-up.

"Can you believe someone left this awesome snake in my car?" he yelled.

Dorothy bit her bottom lip and shook her head. At least Grandma had had the sense to use a fake snake.

After sending Sam up the bleachers to sit with her art teacher, Dorothy raced to the girls' bathroom to find her team.

She was almost to the restrooms when she spotted a group of Pompoms waving signs that said things like, DERBY GIVES YOU SCURVY, SLUGS ARE SLIMY BUGS, and NO KISSES FOR THE HISSES.

How dare they? Dorothy thought, her teeth clenched. What kind of jerks protest roller derby…at a roller derby bout?

Dorothy had done her best to ignore the daily taunts, but now the Pompoms were on her turf. They needed to be taught a lesson.

Dorothy felt her fingers clench around her skate laces. She felt her arm lift the skates above her head. She was about to throw the skates at the Pompoms when a strong hand grabbed her wrist.

"What do you think you're doing?" Gigi said.

"Must…get…Pompoms…" Dorothy grunted, struggling against Gigi's hold.

"Whoa! Calm down, Hulk," Gigi said, confiscating the skates. "Save it for the Cheerbleeders."

"Thank goodness you're here!" It was Jade. Both she and Gigi were already decked out in uniform and pads. "Uh, where's Grandma?"

Dorothy stared blankly at Jade.

"Earth to Dorothy," Jade said, snapping her fingers in front of Dorothy's eyes.

Dorothy blinked. It was as if her brain was moving in slow motion.

"Grandma?" Jade repeated.

"She…parking ticket…police…"

"Oh, great," Gigi said. "Arrested?"

Dorothy nodded.

"Who's going to coach, then?" Jade asked.

Dorothy shrugged.

Just then, the music out on the skate arena grew louder.

"Here," Gigi said, returning Dorothy's skates. "Go get ready. Now! We're on."

A few minutes later, the announcer was calling out names. Dorothy was barely scrambling onto the track as she heard her skate name being called.

She waved at the cheering crowd. Her head felt a lot clearer now that she was skating. Had she really just tried to launch her skates at the Pompoms? Thank goodness Gigi had stopped her. This new, feisty Dorothy was dangerous.

As Dorothy rounded the first corner, she heard a whistle and looked over to see Max waving to her from the middle of the track. He was wearing his black-and-white jersey. Dorothy smiled and waved back. Usually the sight of Max made Dorothy's heart rate skyrocket. Now it was strangely calming. Max was a flirt, but he was also kind and protective. And with Grandma gone, it was nice to know there was someone else looking out for her.

On their last warm-up lap, several Pompoms approached the track and shook protest signs. Gigi turned sideways, flipped up her skirt and waggled her bottom at them. The crowd roared with laughter. Red faced with embarrassment, the Pompoms slunk back to their seats.

Next, the Cheerbleeders were announced. Dorothy shuddered as she watched the older girls race onto the track. The team was dressed in tattered cheerleader costumes. Their faces were painted to look like exposed muscle tissue and bone.

Dorothy's vision blurred. For the first time that night she wondered if they really had a chance to beat the Cheerbleeders. Did the Slugs really belong in the championship? After everything she had done to get to the game tonight, was she just going to make a fool of herself in front of her teachers, classmates, Max, and the Pompoms?

Dorothy looked toward the entrance for the hundredth time in the last minute. Still no Grandma. And no Grandma meant no coach.

A whistle blew, and the first jam was under way.

"Next up! Mayhem! Slugs 'n' Hisses are off to a sloppy start!"

Chapter 25

The Slugs 'n' Hisses gathered in a circle at the edge of the track. Dorothy looked around at the weary, disheartened faces.

Juana fixed her intense, dark eyes on Dorothy. "We needs you," she whispered.

"But I'm skating the best I can," Dorothy said. She couldn't help that the team was falling apart.

"Not for the skating," Juana said. "For the coaching."

"Me? Coach?" Dorothy said, stunned. But that was Grandma's job. She scanned the entrance hall. Still no Grandma.

"You are the logical choice," Geekzilla said. "Your observations have proven accurate."

"They have?" Dorothy said.

Jade looked up from her sweat-drenched towel. "Now that I think of it, Geekzilla's right. You're the perfect coach, Undead."

"Coach! Coach! Coach!" Dinah chanted, and the rest of the team joined in.

"All right, all right!" Dorothy said. "I'll coach." She took a deep breath. "But you all are going to have to listen to me. Okay?"

Everyone nodded. Everyone except Gigi, that is.

"Come on, Gigi. That means you, too," Dorothy said, her voice growing more confident.

"Okay, fine. We'll do it your way," Gigi said. "But you better have a good plan. We're getting eaten alive out there."

"Don't worry," Dorothy said. "I have a plan."

☇☇

"Nice work, team!" Dorothy said. "We're over half-way there!"

"I have to give it to you," Gigi said. "You're a great roller derby coach."

Suddenly the lights flickered and went dark. There were gasps and hoots from the audience.

Dorothy held her breath. Was Eva Disaster going to take her revenge now?

Chapter 26

"I think it's just the halftime show," Jade whispered.

As if on cue, a spotlight appeared in the center of the polished rink floor and Alex skated into it. The room became quiet, except for a few catcalls and some rumbles of laughter.

This is her big surprise, Dorothy thought.

Alex's pink ruffle and sequin costume shimmered like fish scales. Her silky blond ponytail was pulled up into an impossibly tight bun, and her roller skates were brilliantly white. She positioned herself with her legs crossed at the ankle. Her hands rested below her chin, fluttering gently like butterfly wings.

Dorothy felt a sudden urge to giggle, but stopped herself. Alex did look ridiculous, like a sparkly fairy princess taking the stage at a heavy metal concert, but she had some guts, too. What would the Pompoms think?

A single sweet violin note pierced the silence and Alex stretched her arms like wings. Her feet moved like fluid water beneath her, creating circles and spirals that rhythmically expanded and contracted, spinning her body like a leaf on the flowing surface of a stream.

Dorothy held her breath. This was artistic roller-skating? All those times she had seen Alex practicing, she had thought those jumps and leaps were just showy tricks to throw off her team's focus. Now she was seeing something extraordinary. Alex was a powerful skater. Someone who was just as passionate about her brand of roller-skating as Dorothy was about derby.

The single violin grew more spirited, exploring scales with increasing energy, and Alex mirrored the rhythm of the music perfectly. Her movements became sharper and her feet changed directions in quick, precise, sliding steps. As the music built to a crescendo,

Alex turned so she was skating backward. She propelled herself with growing speed, seeming to sense the edge of the skate floor rather than see it with her eyes. The violin reached fever pitch and then froze time with a single, impossibly high note. Alex leapt into the air, spinning her body once, twice, and finally three times before landing smoothly on one skate and eloquently extending the other leg behind her.

The silence that had filled the arena just a moment before erupted into the roar of deafening applause. Dorothy was cheering, too, tears welling at the corners of her eyes. To her surprise, Jade and Gigi were smiling and clapping along with the rest of her team. Even the Pompoms were on their feet, chanting, "Alex! Alex! Alex!" and "Roller-skating rules!"

Alex's face beamed with pride. She waved gracefully, took a bow, and skated off the floor.

Chapter 27

There wasn't any time to find Alex and congratulate her.
There wasn't even time to give her team a final pep talk
or consult the playbook. It was time to jam, and Slugs 'n'
Hisses were still trailing by twelve points. Time to pull
ahead, Dorothy decided.

Time out.

Dorothy and Gigi kneeled next to Jade. She was
curled up in a ball and holding her ankle.

"Make way!" a voice cried. Nurse Boils pushed through
the ring of skaters who had gathered around Jade.

"Stay calm, deary," the nurse said, opening her bag.
Her green eyes looked worried, but she gave Jade a

gap-toothed smile just the same. "We'll have you all fixed up in a minute."

Nurse Boils began untying the laces on the injured foot and Jade cried out in pain.

"Let me through," said a firm female voice. The crowd parted, and a petite Asian woman in a blazer knelt down next to Jade. Her heart-shaped face was a mask of worry.

"Ms. Song?" Gigi yelped.

"Mom?" Jade gasped, trying to focus on the woman.

"It's me, Blossom," the woman said, pushing a strand of hair out of Jade's eyes.

"But how did…" Jade cringed as Nurse Boils pulled her skate off.

"Hush," Jade's mom said. "I've known about this," she gestured to the skate floor, "for a while now."

"But how?" Gigi said.

The woman pointed to a purplish, greenish welt on Jade's leg. "You don't get bruises like this from Cupcake Scouts."

"But…why didn't you stop me?" Jade said through a grimace. Nurse Boils was turning the hurt foot one way, then the other, examining the ankle.

"Because you were happy," she replied. "I haven't seen you happy—really happy—for a long time. Not since before your dad died, anyway."

"So you're not mad at me?" Jade winced.

Ms. Song shook her head. "But I am disappointed that you lied to me."

"I'm sorry, Mom," Jade said. "Really sorry."

"It's my fault, too, Blossom. I realize now that I shouldn't have held you back so much."

"Really?" Jade said.

Her mom nodded. "And if you promise to be honest with me from now on, I promise to give you more freedom. Okay?"

Jade smiled. "Okay."

Nurse Boils pulled a couple of ice packs and a bandage out of her bag and began wrapping Jade's ankle. "Well, it's not a break," she said, "but the ankle is badly sprained. I'm afraid you won't be skating for a few weeks, deary."

"But the game," Jade said. "Who's going to be the jammer?"

Dorothy and Gigi looked at each other. This was a problem. No one else was trained to play that position.

Suddenly Dorothy had an idea. "Hey, can you guys trust me?"

Gigi shrugged. "We made you the coach, didn't we?"

"Uh-huh," Dorothy said. "But you may not like what I have planned."

"Does this idea of yours give us a chance against the Cheerbleeders?" Gigi asked.

Dorothy nodded.

Jade unstrapped her helmet and handed it to Dorothy. "Just do it already!"

ALEX TO THE RESCUE!

WOOSH

Chapter 28

Dorothy felt a tap on her shoulder. She turned to see Grandma smiling at her.

"You're here!"

"Sorry it took me so long," Grandma said. Her nun outfit was wrinkled and her eyes looked tired.

"So you're not in trouble?" Dorothy asked, relieved.

Grandma sighed. "Oh, not anything a few hundred dollars and community service won't take care of."

Dorothy sighed sympathetically.

"You know, Dorothy," Grandma said. "I had some time to think in the back of that police car. I've been a pretty bad role model."

"No you haven't," Dorothy said. Sure, Grandma had almost killed them with her crazy driving several times, but she'd also taught them how to play roller derby. Dorothy had never felt this strong before.

Grandma shook her head. "I promised myself that I was never going to abandon you girls the way I did your mom. And here I go and get myself arrested right when you needed me most. Do you think you can forgive me, Dot?"

"Uh," Dorothy said, suddenly remembering where she had left Dead Betty. "How about I forgive you if you forgive me?" Dorothy said.

Grandma looked confused. "For what?"

Dorothy bit her lip. "You'll see."

Just then Max rolled over to let them know the next jam was about to start.

"So, are you going to coach us now?" Dorothy asked.

"No, hon," Grandma said. "I saw the end of that last jam, and you're a much better coach than I ever was." She pulled out her silver whistle and handed it to Dorothy. "Now go get those Cheerbleeders."

BEFORE JADE WAS INJURED HER SOLO POWER JAM BROUGHT SLUGS 'N' HISSES SEVEN POINTS CLOSER TO THE CHEERBLEEDERS. THERE ARE ONLY TWO MINUTES LEFT IN THE BOUT, AND SLUGS 'N' HISSES ARE TRAILING BY FIVE POINTS. AS THE WHISTLE BLOWS TO START THE LAST JAM, IT'S SLUGS 'N' HISSES' LAST CHANCE FOR THE WIN. TIME TO GET SERIOUS.

HIP CHECK. CHECK MATE! BOOTY VICIOUS KNOCKS CALLOUS ALICE OFF BALANCE AND OFF HER SKATES TO MAKE A SWEET HOLE FOR ALEX.

SHE'S GOT MOM ISSUES ALL RIGHT! DOROTHY TAKES HER AG-GRESSIONS OUT ON BELLE ZEBUB, SENDING HER DOWN AND OUT... OF PLAY!

JUMPIN' JAMMER! ALEX TAKES SKATE DANCING TO A WHOLE NEW LEVEL WHEN SHE JUMPS THE CORNER APEX AND SCORES ANOTHER FIVE POINTS.

GLITTER NEVER LOOKED SO GOOD! ALEX POWERS PAST THE OTHER JAMMER IN THE FINAL SECONDS TO CLINCH THE WIN FOR SLUGS 'N' HISSES.

Chapter 29

The crowd rushed onto the floor, and Dorothy found herself lifted up on her teammates' shoulders. "Undead Redhead! Undead Redhead!" they shouted, bouncing Dorothy up and down.

Dorothy felt exhilarated. She had done it! Her team had played the Cheerbleeders and won, and it had been her coaching that had made their victory possible. What would Mom think now?

Like an apparition, Mom's face appeared at the back of the crowd. At least she thought it was Mom's face. Dorothy was bouncing and spinning too quickly to be sure. When she had circled around again, the face was gone.

It could have been anyone, she thought.

A wave of regret and sadness washed over her as she remembered the fight from earlier that night. Would she ever see Mom again? Or have a normal family again?

All of a sudden she wanted down. She wanted out of Galactic Skate. She wanted to be somewhere alone and quiet and away from the chaos of the cheering crowd.

She tried to get someone's attention, calling and waving her arms, but her team was too caught up in the celebration to notice that Dorothy wanted free. Her eyes darted from face to face. Dinah Mite, Geekzilla, Rolling Thunder, Juana SmackHer, and Dee Tension were all beaming—overjoyed with their win. Gigi was so happy, she had an arm wrapped around Alex's shoulder. Jade was there, too, supported by Grandma and Sam.

Then it dawned on Dorothy. This *was* her family. Was it a normal family? No. Of course not. But was any family really normal? The important thing was that they loved each other, right?

Finally, Dorothy was lowered from her team's shoulders.

Alex's dads had joined the celebration, and Jerry was dabbing his eyes with a monogrammed handkerchief.

"Alexandra, honey," he gushed, "I'm just as proud of you now as when you were crowned Miss Grand National Star Grand Supreme."

Alex blushed as her dads took turns kissing her cheeks.

"And you were quite the coach!" David said, extending a hand to Dorothy.

Dorothy shook David's hand. "Well, we never would have won without your daughter."

Dorothy looked at Alex and bit her lip. "I'm sorry I misjudged you. You were really amazing tonight, Alex."

Alex swept her silky ponytail over her shoulder. "Don't call me Alex."

"Uh, okay," Dorothy said. "Why not?"

"Because I'm the Alexorcist! Every player needs a skate name, right?"

"Darn tootin'," Grandma said, coming up next to Dorothy. "Seems like we got us a real winning team here. Just like the good ol' days…" Grandma's voice trailed off.

Dinah started a round of, *"I'm a roller derby girl! Derby, derby, roller, yeah!"* and the whole team joined in.

Dorothy felt a tap on her shoulder and turned around. She came face-to-face with Max.

"Nice work out there, Dorth." Max was so close, she could feel his sweet, warm breath on her face.

And then it happened. One moment Dorothy was looking up into his twinkling brown eyes and the next moment his soft, full lips were pressed against hers. It was a quick kiss—gentle and a bit awkward, but it made Dorothy's whole body fizz like soda water. The whole world seemed to spin as Dorothy's heart fluttered out of her chest. Her first kiss! Max looked down at her and smiled his crooked smile. Everything was right in the world.

Derby Games

Trivia Training!

Test how much you know about roller derby!

Questions

1. Roller derby started as a roller-skating race event. **True** or **False**
2. Roller derby is only for girls and women. **True** or **False**
3. What was the name of the roller derby movie with Drew Barrymore?
4. You have to be at least 10 years old to play roller derby. **True** or **False**

5. How many roller derby leagues exist in the world today?
    a. More than 500
    b. More than 700
    c. More than 1,000
    d. More than 1,500

6. Which piece of equipment do roller derby athletes NOT wear?
    a. Helmet
    b. Mouth guard
    c. Shoulder pads
    d. Knee pads
    e. Wrist guards

7. It is illegal to hit other skaters in the chest. **True** or **False**

8. You can have the same roller derby name as someone else. **True** or **False**

9. Roller derby is totally fake. **True** or **False**

10. You have to be a good athlete to play roller derby. **True** or **False**

Answers

1. **True!** Roller-skating endurance races started as early as 1884! The term "derby" was first used in a media story in 1922, and Leo Seltzer created the official sport in 1935.

2. **False!** There are at least 40 all-men's roller derby leagues, and sometimes they play the girls!

3. *Whip It!* came out in 2009 and starred Ellen Page, Kristen Wiig, and Drew Barrymore.

4. **False!** Many junior leagues let kids as young as six years old play the sport.

5. There are more than **1,500** men's, women's, recreational, and junior leagues in the world.

6. Roller derby players often hit with their shoulders, but they **don't wear shoulder pads**.

7. **False!** Hitting a skater in the sternum with your shoulder is an awesome hit! But hard to do!

8. **False!** There is a worldwide website called Two Evils that lists all roller derby names. You have to get approval from the skater if your name is very similar.

9.   **False!** Roller derby is a totally real, full contact sport, with strict rules and penalties.

10.   **False!** Roller derby can make athletes out of non-athletes. All you have to do is love to skate.

Visit us at www.dorothysderby.com for more trivia fun!

The Name Game!

Create your own roller derby name!

For Your First Name

Take the first three or four letters of your first name.

Attach the name of your favorite animal to it.

For example:

Meghan/Dog = Megdog

Alece/Tiger = Aletiger

Emily/Cat = Emicat

For Your Second Name (Unless you love having just one name!)

Choose one of the following for the first half of your last name:

For first names A–D: Roller (or Roll)

For first names E–H: Skate

For first names I–L: Killa

For first names M–P: Wheel

For first names Q–T: Speed

For first names U–W: Hit

For first names X–Z: Track

Attach your favorite movie character to it. (Add yours if you don't see it listed!)

Villain

Queen

Princess

Star

Geek

Bully

Pal

Bestie

Here's How You'd Roll!

Meghan/Dog/Queen = Megdog Wheel Queen

Alece/Tiger/Villain = Aletiger Roller Villain

Emily/Cat/Geek = Emicat Skate Geek

Visit us at www.dorothysderby.com for more fun ways to find your true roller derby identity!

Read on for a special
sneak peek at Dorothy's
next derby adventure.

Chapter 1

"You okay, Dorth?" Max said, squeezing Dorothy's hand.

Dorothy just stared up into Max's chocolate brown eyes. Words weren't coming. From the tiptop of her curly red hair right down to her hand-me-down roller skates, Dorothy was buzzing with delight. She wasn't even twelve yet, and she had just been kissed! She had thought the night couldn't get any better after coaching her team, the Slugs 'n' Hisses, to a win at the Halloween championship bout, but here she was, hand in hand with the boy of her dreams.

Floating on a cloud of bliss, Dorothy was barely aware of the roller rink under her feet or her nearby team chanting, "I'm a roller derby girl. Derby, derby, roller, yeah!"

And there was another sound too, like a squeal. But not a happy squeal. More like a metallic screech, actually. And it was growing louder.

Suddenly, Dorothy's gaze shot upward and her bliss vanished, replaced instead with heart pounding terror.

"Get off the floor!" she screamed. "NOW!"

Dorothy's team stopped chanting and turned to look at her with puzzled faces.

"Frappit," Dorothy said, dropping Max's hand. She rocketed towards her team, her arms waving frantically above her head. "Move it!"

"You heard your coach!" Grandma Sally yelled. Unaware that her sexy nun costume was riding up dangerously high, Grandma hooked Jade by the arm and pulled her towards the bleachers. The tight fishnet stockings made Grandma's backside look like a pair of misshapen waffles.

"Ouch, Grandma! Easy," Jade complained, hopping on one foot. "My ankle, remember?"

The next few seconds were a blur of confusion. The clack and swoosh of skate wheels, the cries of "run!" from the few remaining fans standing in the bleachers, and above it all, a metallic banshee shriek growing louder by the moment.

In the chaos, Dorothy realized she had lost track of Sam. Cold fingers of panic wrapped around Dorothy's throat and squeezed. Her nine-year-old sister had been there just a minute ago, chanting and celebrating with her team. Where was she now?

Then it happened. With a bang like a gun going off...

Acknowledgments

This book is dedicated to roller derby athletes everywhere, to the misfits, dorks, geeks, class presidents, ex-cheerleaders, prom queens, and class clowns that roller derby loves. You know who you are. Because roller derby doesn't care how big or little you are, where you come from, or who you know. It loves everybody.

Special thanks to everyone who rolled with us and helped us jam through this process with winning success. And especially to our juniors: Sawyer, Claire, Hannah, Dominic, and Lilly.

Love, Meghan and Alece

About the Authors

Meghan Dougherty is a roller derby–playing wife and mom and owner of a small PR agency. Since 2007, Meghan has been entertained and inspired by her roller derby sisters, who are some of the smartest, most independent, and funniest women she knows. Alece Birnbach has been drawing girls her whole life. From her fine art to her commercial illustrations—found on products across the country—Alece has been inspired by the diversity and complexity of the feminine form and spirit. Friends for more than twenty years, Meghan and Alece share a free spirit and entrepreneurial quest for adventure. Together they hatched a genius plan to combine Alece's gift of capturing the essence of sassy girl power with Meghan's roller derby story and adventures, to create a book series for girls. All to give tween girls a taste of the fun, fierceness, friendship, empowerment, and positive body image that the sport of roller derby brings to women from six to sixty.